LONE STAR HEROES

The Hidden Treasure
of the Chisos

LONE STAR HEROES

The Hidden Treasure of the Chisos

Patrick Dearen

Illustrations by Alan McCuller

Republic of Texas Press
Plano, Texas

Library of Congress Cataloging-in-Publication Data

Dearen, Patrick.
 The hidden treasure of the Chisos / Patrick Dearen.
   p.   cm. -- (Lone Star heroes)
 Summary: In the late 1800s when the words of a dying Indian lead
 twelve-year-old Fish and his stepbrother into the Chisos Mountains
 in search of a lost gold mine, they face many dangers, including a
 band of Apache warriors, one of whom turns out to be a trusted friend.
 ISBN 1-55622-829-5
 [1. Gold mines and mining--Fiction.   2. Apache Indians--Fiction.
 3. Indians of North America--Texas--Fiction.   4. Texas--Fiction.]
 I. Title. II. Series.

 PZ7.D3516 Hi   2001
 [Fic]--dc21   2001019703
                                                   CIP

Republic of Texas Press is an imprint of Wordware Publishing, Inc.
No part of this book may be reproduced in any form or by
any means without permission in writing from
Wordware Publishing, Inc.

Printed in the United States of America

ISBN 1-55622-829-5
10 9 8 7 6 5 4 3 2 1
0104

All inquiries for volume purchases of this book should be addressed to
Wordware Publishing, Inc., at 2320 Los Rios Boulevard, Plano, Texas 75074.
Telephone inquiries may be made by calling:
(972) 423-0090

For the two Wesleys in my life:
my grandfather, Alma Wesley Dearen (1889-1964)
and my son, Wesley Dearen

My life is so much richer because of both of you.

Other books in the Lone Star Heroes series:

Comanche Peace Pipe
by Patrick Dearen

On the Pecos Trail
by Patrick Dearen

The Lone Star Heroines series:

Secrets in the Sky
by Melinda Rice

Fire on the Hillside
by Melinda Rice

Messenger on the Battlefield
by Melinda Rice

Glossary

booger—(noun) anything worthy of a cowhand's fear; (verb) to scare.

boogered—(adjective) scared.

breechcloth—(noun) a cloth worn to cover the hips.

bronc—(noun) a horse that is not very gentle.

buoy—(verb) to lift or hold up.

chigo-na-ay—(Apache, noun) sun.

gig—(verb) to spur a horse.

hobble—(verb) to tie the legs together so an animal or person can walk but not run.

hooraw—(verb) to tease good-naturedly or celebrate wildly; (noun) the act of teasing or celebrating wildly.

intchi-dijin—(Apache, noun) black wind.

ittindi—(Apache, noun) lightning.

izze-nantan—(Apache, noun) medicine man.

just deserts—(noun) what a person has earned through his actions.

ka-chu—(Apache, noun) jackrabbit.

kah—(Apache, noun) arrow.

nock—(verb) to place a notched arrow in a bowstring.

pesh-litzogue—(Apache, noun) yellow iron or gold.

pindah-lickoyee—(Apache, noun) white eyes or white person.

pitch—(verb) to jump upward with stiff forelegs and fall back suddenly; said of a horse.

pollywog—(noun) nickname for a tadpole.

shied—(verb) past tense of "shy": to jump as though startled.

Shis-Inday—(Apache, noun) men of the woods; Apaches' name for themselves.

shoz-dijiji—(Apache, noun) black bear.

stompede—(noun) a cowhand's way of saying "stampede."

swan—(verb) to declare, as in "I swan."

Usen—(Apache, noun) God.

wrangler—(noun) the cowboy responsible for taking care of the saddle horse herd.

yah-tats-an—(Apache, phrase) now it is dead, said of a killed animal.

yandestan—(Apache, noun) sky.

yay-hoo—(noun) yahoo; a person from the backwoods who would seem crude and out of place in a city.

yoke—(verb) to put a harness on an animal.

· ∘) 〰 (∘ ·

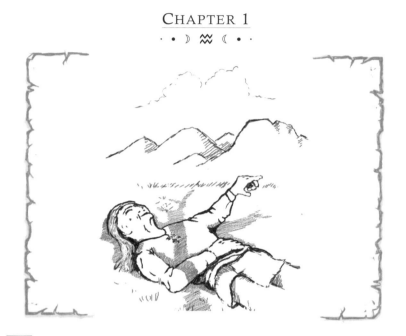

CHAPTER 1

Twelve-year-old Fish Rawlings' skin was crawling.

He and his best friend Gid had dragged the shriveled old Indian with the long, yellow-white hair in under a shrubby tarbush. It was the best shade they could find on this rocky point. But the wind-blown leaves still let plenty of searing midday sun through.

The rays found the sickly Apache's troubled eyes and a tortured face as cracked as an old saddlebag. The sunlight danced across his leather shirt and breechcloth and down rugged moccasins that reached almost to his knees. But all Fish could see was the wrinkled hand that pointed to the faraway Chisos Mountains. Jagged and lonely, the peaks rose out of a great sea known as the Chihuahuan Desert or Big Bend of Texas.

"The mountains cry—don't you hear? The cradle of life bleeds—can't you see?"

1

Fish had heard the Chisos were haunted. Now he had reason to believe it. Between moans, the aged Apache had been talking. He had whispered words Fish hadn't understood, but the gestures had been plain. Years ago Fish's pa had taught him Indian sign language. It had come in handy at times, but now the young cowboy almost wished he had never learned it. If he hadn't understood the Apache's every sign, his skin wouldn't be crawling the way it was.

Just hovering over a painted Apache with a wicked knife at his belt was scary enough. After all, this was 1869, and Apaches were on the prowl for horses and scalps. Right now Fish was only a mile from the Rio Grande and the Mexico border. Just a half-day's ride across the river was the Sierra del Carmen, the last stronghold of the Chisos Apaches. Twice already they had raided his Uncle Guy's Texas ranch on the far side of the Chisos Mountains.

Twelve-year-old Gid was whirling left and right, searching the lechuguilla stalks. Like Fish, he dressed the part of a cowhand. He wore a sweat-stained hat, linsey-woolsey shirt, duck pants, and high-topped boots with spurs. With those deep dimples in his freckled face, he could usually grin a prairie dog out of its hole. But right now he looked mighty worried.

"What's he a-tellin' you, Fish?" he asked.

Oro, as the old Indian called himself, had told Fish plenty—ninety-two years' worth, to be exact. It sure hadn't been what Fish expected when they had ridden upon him a few minutes before. Oro had been sprawled in the blazing sun, far from his paint pony. He had been clutching his chest and fighting for breath. The boys had tended him the best they could. But it was plain to see that the old Apache had about reached his end.

"I know he's sick and all," added Gid, still studying the desert with near-panic. "But if there's one Indian around, they's liable to be more. What if one of them Apache barbers shows up? We gotta do somethin'!"

But Oro had only one thing left to tell. The anguished eyes suddenly seemed to stare deep into Fish's soul as the quaking hand pointed again to the Chisos. When the old Indian began to speak in signs once more, his struggles were those of a dying man.

"I give you the mountains' secret—just you! They bleed, and only you can stop it! Go! Do what I should've done! Go now!"

When Oro closed his eyes and his head fell to one side, Fish knew it was over. Or was it just beginning? With a shudder, he turned to Gid and found him staring down at the old Apache. Gid was Fish's cousin, but he was also his brother now. Gid had lost his mother young, and Fish had lost his pa just a year ago. When Fish's mother had married his Uncle Guy last month, the boys had found themselves in a real family again.

But none of that seemed very reassuring right now.

"We can't help him no more, can we," said Gid.

Fish turned to the Chisos Mountains. Now they seemed more than just a mighty island jutting out of the desert. They seemed downright eerie.

"Maybe there's one thing we can do," he whispered, feeling a sudden chill.

"Huh?"

Fish turned back to Gid. "There's a lot of rocks around. Let's bury him best we can and get out of here. This place gives me the creeps."

Fish would have felt even jumpier if he had known what was on the nearby ridge.

Watching their every move from behind cacti and desert shrubs were eight sets of fierce Apache eyes—and one set not so fierce.

· • ⟩ ∼ ⟨ • ·

A half-hour later the boys rode upstream, trailing along a rocky bluff high above the muddy Rio Grande. They had come all this way looking for horses that had strayed from the Rawlings outfit, the family ranch around on the other side of the Chisos Mountains. But now the boys had more important things on their minds.

"Wha'd that ol' Indian tell you?" Gid asked over the strike of hoofs. "You looked white as a sheet back there. Still do."

Fish nodded to the distant Chisos. "Ever hear Uncle Guy—I mean *Papa Guy*—tell about a lost mine up there?"

"The Spanish diggin's in the Chisos? Why, sure. He heard all about it from his Mexican hands."

"Wha'd they tell him?"

"You've heard it, same as me. Back in the 1700s—didn't Papa say '77?—the Spaniards had 'em a fort right across the river. San Vicente, I think. Anyhow, story is they made slaves out of the Chisos Apaches. Marched 'em blindfolded across the desert to the Chisos Mountains. Spaniards had 'em a mine up there, and they made them Indians work it for 'em. Found a lot of gold and silver, Papa said. Somehow the mine got lost over the years. That's been what? A hundred years?"

"Ninety-two," said Fish. "You believe any of that, Gid?"

"I dunno. Why?"

"That old Apache back there said he was one of the slaves—the last one left."

Gid drew rein, stunned. "You're kiddin'!"

Fish held his horse and looked straight into his best friend's eyes. "I ain't, but I don't know if Oro was or not."

"Oro?"

"That's what he called hisself. Don't that mean *gold* in Spanish?"

"Maybe. He tell you anything else about the mine?"

"Yeah. How to find it."

Gid's jaw dropped. For long seconds he just stared at Fish. "Why would he want to go and do that? You ain't even Indian."

Fish took a deep breath and studied the faraway mountains. "I reckon he had his reasons."

"You believe him?"

"Pa always said if a man's dyin', he don't have any call to lie."

"A gold mine!" exclaimed Gid. "A real gold mine! You think you can take us to it? Papa's sure facin' some hard times. He's up at that Yankee fort in New Mexico right now, doin' his best to get a beef contract. If he don't get some money for them steers of his mighty quick, his whole ranch is liable to go belly up."

Fish sure didn't want to see that. Papa Guy had been awfully good to him and his ma. He had assumed a lot of extra burden by taking them in. He was a good man with plenty of love to give, just like Fish's pa had been. For all that and more, Fish owed it to his uncle to help out any way he could.

But that's not what Oro had intended when he had told him the Chisos' darkest secret. Still, what good was gold or silver if nobody could ever spend it?

"This is Friday, ain't it, Gid? Tell me what Sunday is."

"Sunday's the day after tomorrow. Sunday always comes the day after Saturday, and Saturday's always the day after Friday."

"I know that, silly billy. I mean, ain't day after tomorrow Easter Sunday?"

"Why, sure. I thought you knowed that."

Fish gigged his horse. "Come on! We got our work cut out for us! We got to find that old Spanish fort before sunup Sunday!"

"Why? What for? Hey, wait for me!"

CHAPTER 2

· •) ≈ (• ·

"What's so special about this place? Ain't nothin' here but a bunch of mud walls."

Gid was right. They had roamed the Mexico side of the river a day and a half looking for this old fort. They had dared a blazing sun and crawling rattlers and Apache scalp knives. But Presidio de San Vicente was just a crumbling ruin on a sun-baked knoll a mile off the river. Meanwhile, twenty crow-flight miles northwest, above a camel's hump ridge well into Texas, the Chisos Mountains brooded as mysterious as ever.

About the only decent walls left were those of the roofless chapel. But they were exactly what Fish was looking for.

As soon as he dismounted, he ran inside. He was trying to figure out where the original doorway had been. There were so many breaches now it was hard to tell. But only one notch opened to the Chisos.

Gid was too tired to climb off his roan horse. "Mama Elizabeth's gonna go to worryin' about us," he said wearily. "I thought we was gonna go look for that lost mine."

"We are," said Fish, studying the creosote that grew out of the discolored melt-down. "This is where we gotta start. See that ol' doorway? The one facin' Texas and the Chisos? That's where we gotta be standin' come sunup tomorrow."

"What for?" Gid asked, slumping in the saddle. Whenever Gid got tired, he got grumpy. And he was mighty tired right now. "Ain't the sun gonna come up ever'where else too?"

By now Fish was standing right in the opening. He pointed just opposite the setting sun to a great, red-splashed band across the horizon.

"Look over yonder east of the Chisos. See what a wall the Sierra del Carmen makes? See all them teeth it's got along its ridge?"

"So? I got teeth too. Just got precious little to sink 'em into out here. Serves me right, goin' off on a wild goose chase this-away with you."

"You wanna find treasure or not?"

"Sure I do. But sourdough biscuits and fried steak sounds just about as good right now."

"All right then. The sun will be comin' up right over the Carmen Mountains, and its first rays will shoot right between those highest teeth."

"So?"

"So when they do, they're gonna hit the Chisos—smack-dab where that lost mine is. Oro told me so. He come back here once and seen it."

Suddenly Gid lost his hunger and found new energy. He straightened in the saddle, touched spurs to his horse, and took the roan in a lope right up inside the crumbling walls.

"Let me see! Let me see!" he cried.

If Fish hadn't reeled back, Gid's horse would have bowled him over.

"Whoa, boy! Whoa!" Fish cried, to Gid and the horse both. "I said sun-*up*, not sun-*down*!"

· ·) ≋ (· ·

As night choked the ruins with heavy shadows, Fish slept where men long dead had walked.

He tossed and turned, because the half-melted walls were as ghostly as the Spanish empire had been mighty. In his dreams he didn't even seem to be Fish anymore. Instead, he was the young Apache boy Oro, who would carry a secret through his long, hard life.

He was outside his parents' lodge in a desert hideaway. He was watching scowling Spaniards with deadly lances storm the Apache camp on war horses. The invaders wore dark, flat-brimmed hats and spurs with big rowels. They had thick shields and arrow-proof leather vests.

War cries rang out as warriors ran for their weapons. They had been caught off-guard, but they were brave and determined. Their metal-tipped arrows flew and their gleaming knives flashed. Still, their weapons were no match for muskets and pistols. The battle was swift and the outcome never in doubt.

When it was over, the Spanish victors tied their captives' hands and hobbled their legs. They yoked them like oxen and marched them away into slavery. The prisoners were mere boys like Oro, and full-grown men like his father. Defeated but not beaten, they trudged without a whimper under the sting of the Spaniards' whips.

The lash found his father's shoulders often. But Oro never saw him flinch. Instead, Oro read a building hatred in the warrior's proud eyes, as well as an unspoken truth.

Someday the Spanish devils would pay for this.

Fish awoke with a start to the eerie sound of bells tolling.

He bolted upright in the dark, his heart suddenly hammering. It had been nearly a century since bells had rung in this old church. He whirled and found the shadows thicker than ever. But now the night seemed quiet, except for his own rapid breathing and Gid's snoring.

Still, Fish was covered with chill bumps. What was he getting himself into?

"Hey, Gid, Gid—you hear somethin'?" he whispered. Fish was nudging his cousin and searching the dark at the same time.

"Huh? I'm tired, Papa. Let me sleep some more, Punk."

"I ain't your papa. Or Punk neither, that sorry rascal. Come on. Wake up, Gid. I heard somethin'."

"Huh? What?"

"A racket. Shook me plum' out of my bedroll."

Gid raised his head sleepily. "I don't hear nothin'. You must've been dreamin'."

Fish still couldn't calm his hammering heart. "Yeah," he tried to assure himself. He studied the gloomy walls that suddenly seemed to crowd so close. "I . . . I must've been dreamin'."

He lay back, feeling the panic race through him. He edged as close to Gid as he could get, then scooted even closer. If anything haunted these ruins, maybe the two of them together would look too big to tangle with.

"What the dickens you doin'?" asked Gid. "You're just about layin' on top of me."

"Ju-just cold, I reckon," said Fish, still scanning the walls anxiously.

"Cold? Why, you could near' fry an egg without any fire tonight."

Fish withdrew an inch or two, just enough so Gid wouldn't complain. Soon, Gid lapsed into sleep again. But Fish stayed wide-eyed. He didn't know if he would ever sleep again. Shivering, he lay there under a star-studded sky and seemed to live Oro's story once more.

The fort's walls were strong again, strong enough to hold a proud race captive. Day after day at the cruel whims of their masters, Oro and his people toiled under a broiling sun. From dawn until dusk, they forged horseshoes and trinkets, spurs, and shiny conchos. And always it was from the silver or yellow metals the white men had such a liking for.

Every moon when the gates opened for a dusty burro train, the days grew longer. There were forty jack-loads of ore to cast into heavy bars and stack in a barred storehouse.

Even as the sweat poured, the guards denied the captives anything but water and corn meal. A daily bowl of porridge was enough to keep a boy like Oro alive, but not a grown warrior. As the weeks passed, his parents withered away. All too soon, their skin hung loosely over their bones.

One day the guards marched Oro and the men through the gates. There was a great hole outside and a winding path leading down. At the bottom, the guards briefly held each warrior at a dark tunnel extending into the rock. No more than six feet high, it seemed to point straight toward the Rio Grande and the Chisos Mountains.

When Oro reached the shaft, the Spaniards did what they had done to every captive before him. They tied his arms, hobbled his legs, and slipped a blindfold over his eyes. As everything went black, Oro suddenly knew more than he had ever expected. If his captors wanted to keep this route such a secret, it had to concern the shiny metal they valued more than human lives.

Rough hands prodded him inside, and Oro was on his way to a hidden mine that would haunt him all his years.

Fish rolled over to face the Sierra del Carmen through a breach in the wall. A red glow hugged the mountains' broad and saw-like crest.

"Gid! Gid, get up!" he cried, shaking his cousin. "The sun's comin' up! We gotta be in that door a-watchin'! We gotta find us a lost mine!"

CHAPTER 3

· •)) ≋ ((• ·

Fish stood in the jagged "V" that once was the chapel door. In the distance, the Chisos range was a ragged shadow against the pre-dawn sky. At any time of day, the mountains always looked wild and weird. But in the dark, they also seemed spooky and menacing. Their spires and rock fists stared Fish in the face like misty spirits rising from a century-old grave.

"Say, Fish?"

Fish jumped like a just-mounted horse on a frosty morning.

"Don't be sneakin' up thataway, Gid!" he exclaimed without turning. "You're bad as Punk! I doggone near played snake and come out of my skin!"

"Gee whiz, I ain't sneakin' nowhere. Been right here all the time. And anyhow, I couldn't hold a candle to Punk when it comes to playin' pranks. So when's that sun comin' up? This ol' wind's kickin' up the dust and makin' my nose itch."

Fish never shifted his gaze from the Chisos. "Well, I ain't scratchin' it for you. I'm busy a-watchin'. We got us one chance, and that's it."

Soon, a soft light filled the eastern sky, and Fish allowed himself an occasional glance at it. Every crag in the Sierra del Carmen's backbone stood out boldly. El Pico, the Carmen's highest point, seemed to watch over the desert and its secrets like a guardian. Before much longer, the rim's sharp notches became bright with the coming dawn.

"Any second now!" cried Fish, gluing his eyes on the Chisos.

"Come on, sun!" urged Gid. "Show us the... *a-choo!*"

Gid's sneeze forced his eyes shut for a moment. But it was long enough to miss the sun's first rays bursting through the del Carmen's toothy ridge.

"Holy smokes!" exclaimed Fish.

"What is it?" cried Gid.

For a mere instant, the rising sun had burned against a single bump on the Chisos skyline. The knot looked almost white, as if it was a rocky butte on one of the chief mountains. On its left was a smaller peak. On past that was a sudden cut that had to mark a deep canyon.

Fish saw other details too. But that special bump was what seized his attention, even after the show was over.

"That's it!" he cried. "Oro told me how it was, and that's gotta be it!"

"Where at? I don't see nothin'! The sun's lightin' up ever mountain over there!"

"You missed it! You sneezed and missed it!"

"You mean I gotta wait a whole year to see it again?" asked Gid. "What kind of clue's that? We can't wait around here a whole year!"

"We don't have to, silly billy! I seen ever'thing there was to see! Come on, let's get them horses saddled up! We got some ridin' to do!"

· • ⟩ ≋ ⟨ • ·

As they rode out, Fish was drawn to a broad sinkhole just outside the ruins. For the past two days he had been trying to judge the truth of Oro's story. So far everything was just as the old Apache had described. Now he wondered if there was a tunnel down in that hole. If so, then maybe, just maybe, he and Gid really were on the trail to treasure. Anyway, it only made sense that the fort would have an escape passage in case of Indian attack.

But this pit didn't tell him much. It was only a few feet deep, and the sides were all sloughed. If there had ever been a shaft down there that had led to the river, it had long-since caved in.

The boys were still peering over the rim when a horse nickered in the distance.

Fish whirled, searching the desert. He wasn't sure where the sound had come from. But Gid suddenly was pointing excitedly into the sunrise.

"There he is!" Gid exclaimed.

Sure enough, on a yucca-covered rise three hundred yards away, a rider was framed by the rising sun. Fish went cold. The sun was blinding, but a horseman could mean only one thing here in Mexico—Indians! And this warrior had his horse in a gallop and was headed straight their way!

"Let's get out of here!" cried Fish.

The boys touched spurs to their horses and they were off, fleeing for the Rio Grande and Texas a mile away. The hoofs were pounding, and so was Fish's heart. Eighteen months ago on the Concho River, he had made the ride of his life in escaping a band of Comanches. A cat in his fix would have used up eight of its nine lives. That sure didn't leave much to work with now that he had another enemy on his tail.

The dust flew as the boys pushed their ponies through the shin-high lechuguilla. The green clusters stood like curved knives waiting to stick. Their horses broke through shrubby acacia and skeleton-like cholla and plunged down a sharp bank covered with prickly pear. They hit a gravelly wash at bottom, then a steep and rocky rise. But Fish was riding a big bay with lots of muscle, and he could feel the animal's strength as it carried him up.

With Gid right behind, he topped out on a brief flat dotted with shrubby creosote. Thirty yards farther, the land fell away suddenly. Just beyond was the Rio Grande, brown with silt and white with frothy water. From here it looked mighty uninviting, and so did that sharp bank.

Still, Fish didn't draw rein until he was at its edge. Fifteen feet straight down was a rolling river that looked as wicked as the dickens. It had come on a huge rise since the day before. Its muddy water rushed by like a war horse at full gallop. But Texas and their best hope of escape lay just beyond.

Fish wheeled his bay to find Gid pulling rein.

"What are we gonna do?" Gid cried. "Hair-cuttin's Papa's business, not no Indian's!"

Fish looked past his cousin's floppy hat and saw their foe's dust hanging against the rising sun.

"He's gainin' ground! We gotta cross somehow!"

Fish turned his bay upstream and spurred it into flight along the high bank. He had to find a way down! He kept the horse in a gallop for two hundred yards before a deep gully cut across his path. Twenty feet wide and lined with spiny tasajillo, it had banks as sharp as the river.

He pulled up. The arroyo was like a dry moat. A horse would have needed wings to cross it.

"He's got us trapped!" exclaimed Gid as he reined up alongside.

It sure looked like it, thought Fish. There was an impossible gully in front of them, a raging river at their side, and a charging Indian behind. But Fish had lived through a cattle stampede before, not to mention a killer sandstorm and several horse wrecks. Shoot, he had even faced a cyclone over on the Pecos. He wasn't a boy who gave up easily.

He spun his horse toward the Rio Grande. "The river! We gotta do it, Gid!"

"But I done had my bath this week!"

"You want a haircut too?"

It was all the reminder Gid needed. "What are you waitin' on! Let's take these ponies for a swim!"

At the bank's edge, Fish hesitated. Between his horse's ears, he could see a lot of wild, frothy water a dozen feet below. With that deadly current, he wouldn't have bet a plug nickel on their chances.

"He's right on our tail!" hollered Gid.

With a quick prayer, Fish plunged his horse toward the churning rapids.

CHAPTER 4

· •) ≈ (• ·

Seventeen-year-old Punk was an experienced wrangler, but he was still just a big kid. He delighted in playing pranks even more than he loved to eat. And no other cowhand with the Rawlings Ranch could gobble up food the way rail-thin Punk could.

That's why he had a grin the size of Texas as he rode through broken country on the Mexico side of the Rio Grande at sunup. He was planning his next prank and thinking about all the beans he would feast on when he got back to the ranch. The only trouble was, he had to overtake Fish and Gid first. And the Rawlings boys had left a pretty tough trail to follow.

A one-eyed bat could have tracked them from headquarters to the river. But as soon as their trail had crossed into Mexico, it had zigzagged like a dizzy donkey. Punk didn't know what those boys were up to. But he would sure hooraw them about it once he caught up.

Punk was crossing a deep, winding wash when he suddenly heard a sound that made his hair stand on end. He turned toward a sharp bend thirty yards to his right. Something was around there, headed his way! He could hear the crunch of hoofs against gravel!

His jaw hadn't finished dropping when several horses spilled into view.

Mustangs! Maybe they were just wild mustangs!

He sure wasn't going to wait around to find out. This was Apache country, and Punk liked his hair just the way it was.

He gigged his sorrel horse, and the animal bolted toward the far bank. Its hoofs dug into the steep rise, but the footing was poor. He could feel the animal's struggles as it slipped and slid.

Time seemed to stand still, but his thoughts were on a breakneck pace. *Gotta ride like the dickens, Punk, ol' boy! Can't this ol' pony go any faster? What's the matter with the clabberhead? This sorry thing couldn't out-run a three-legged ol' donkey!*

He was still several feet from the top when an Indian rider burst into sight down the arroyo. The Apache was just a boy, not yet a teen-ager, and he was driving seven horses up the wash from the river.

Punk's eyes grew as wide as full moons. Now he was *really* scared. An Apache's face, even a boy's, looked so fierce. The youth had dark, narrow eyes that seemed to glare beneath overhung brows. His nose was like a hawk's beak, and his cheekbones thrust out. The heavy lines that angled up from the corners of his mouth seemed to freeze his face in a scowl. The war paint on his forehead and cheeks made him look even more savage.

But that wasn't all that alarmed Punk. He could see the Indian's war turban, or fur head wrap, with its hummingbird, oriole, quail, and eagle feathers. He could make out the single-arc bow and four feathered arrows in a deer-hide quiver over his shoulder. He could almost feel their points tickling his ribs.

Maybe the Apache hadn't lifted his eyes to him yet, but Punk saw plenty of reason to ride like blazes.

The sorrel burst out on top, and Punk put spurs to it. The horse flew across an elevated flat heavy with lechuguilla and yucca. He glanced back into the rising sun and wondered how many warriors were behind that boy and about to give chase.

He patted the sorrel on the neck. "Run, you ol' nag! Run!" he urged. "Give ol' Punk ever'thing you got!"

Luckily, the sorrel had plenty of vigor after a night of rest. Its hoofs drummed like distant thunder as it carried Punk toward mud-colored ruins three hundred yards away.

Suddenly he saw dust rising ahead and a pair of riders racing away from the old adobe walls. He couldn't tell much about them at a distance, but he didn't figure them for Indians. They seemed to have the same idea he had—make tracks fast for Texas!

He cut his horse and took in after them, wishing he were in the lead instead of them.

The sorrel ate up ground in a hurry. As Punk neared the Rio Grande, he could see the riders drawing rein on the high bank just two hundred yards upstream. Then he plunged down into a wash and lost sight of them. As soon as he topped out near the river, he saw the two jump their ponies off into the raging flood.

He spun to the young sun. He didn't see any Indians, but that didn't mean there weren't any back there. Even now, they could be in a nearby arroyo, ready to pop out and bend their bows.

But he sure didn't like the idea of doing what those horsemen had done. That drop-off was awfully high, and a rider could lose his grip in a dive like that. If he did, he might as well kiss thoughts of any more beans goodbye. A horse might have the strength to swim that torrent, but he didn't much figure a man would.

Well downstream of the point where the riders had jumped their horses into the river, Punk pulled up at bank's edge. The rapids below looked scarier than ever. But behind him was at least one Apache who could be itching for trouble.

Whirling to the hanging dust at his tail, Punk weighed the danger below against the danger behind.

· • ⟩ ≋ ⟨ • ·

It all happened so fast that things went from day to night in an instant.

Fish's horse hit the rushing river with a jarring impact that threw him across the bay's neck. Suddenly the world was nothing but bubble-filled water. He was still in the saddle, but the horse was rolling with him. He lost his grip on the horn. One foot floated free, but the other drove through the stirrup and caught.

Suddenly boy and horse were tumbling wildly, captured by a current stronger than either. Fish's father had tried to tell him once how powerful a raging river could be. This was sure a bad time to figure it out for himself.

He came up long enough to gasp for air in the foam and take heart. Then the bay dragged him under again. For second after awful second, they went bobbing downstream that way, a boy and a horse tossed about by an angry river.

Fish had never been so scared.

He was hung to a horse and couldn't get free! He was helpless in churning rapids that were drowning him! Air! He had to have air!

At a bend, the current swept them against the high Mexico bank. Fish's pinned leg caught the brunt of the impact. If he had been above water, he would have yelled with pain. Then he and the bay slid away and he was on the surface long enough to glimpse something high on the point ahead.

It was a rider—a cowboy! And he was twirling a rope over his head!

The struggling horse yanked Fish under once more. When the boy popped up again he saw a loop flying out. He reached for it and missed. But somehow it dropped straight over the bay's neck.

Fish's life was on the line. He sure hoped the cowboy had a stout horse. This rampaging river wasn't going to slow down for anybody!

The bay floated headlong downstream and hit the end of the rope with a tremendous jerk. Fish, his boot still fast to the stirrup, went right over the animal's head. But suddenly all hope was gone. Upstream he saw the cowboy and his horse hit the water with a tremendous splash. The force had dragged them right off the crumbling bluff!

Now two horses were surging downstream, joined by a snake-like rope that might drown them all.

Fish had sure missed his pa since he had lost him a year ago. Now it looked like he would be able to see him again a lot sooner than he had ever expected.

Suddenly he was free of the stirrup. He had a chance! He could put into practice what his father had taught him back in that East Texas swimming hole!

Fish dug his arms into the water and kicked like a stubborn mule. The flow was as strong as ever. But at least he could keep his head above water. Even so, it was a hard current to fight. It drove him on around a bend and across the river at an angle. There was a low bank up ahead on the Texas side. With the river running so high, the bank's carrizo and seep willow were standing in water.

The flow carried Fish through flooded reeds and straight for an overhanging willow. A couple of higher limbs looked sturdy. But the lower branches were so limber they couldn't even support their own weight. Their ends were draped in the rushing water and bouncing to its tug. He just hoped they weren't as flimsy as they looked.

He grabbed a drooping branch and braced himself for a fight with the river.

· •) ≈ (• ·

CHAPTER 5

Child-of-the-Waters was scared, but he would never have admitted it. An Apache novice, or beginning warrior, couldn't afford to show fear. He couldn't flinch even if he was alone and facing his first enemy. It was true that a novice was allowed only four blunt arrows for hunting. But even a lack of weapons could be no excuse for showing fright.

Still, Punk had startled him. Child-of-the-Waters had lifted his gaze to the hoofbeats and watched the young cowboy spur his horse up the bank. The *pindah-lickoyee*, or white eyes, was gone now. But Child-of-the-Waters still had a hard time catching his breath.

He had just finished watering the horses at the Rio Grande, and now he had to hurry them back to camp. He had to tell Alchesay and Loco and the other warriors who were spying on the old adobe walls. They believed that the two white boys at the

21

ruins were alone. They believed that the boys were unaware that Chisos Apaches were so close. Now, all that may have changed.

Suddenly the war party's plans were threatened. Alchesay was dead-set on secretly trailing the boys who had heard Oro's last breaths. Maybe Oro had told the boys something he had refused to tell these warriors. Maybe he had told them where to find *pesh-litzogue*, the yellow iron in the Chisos.

Child-of-the-Waters pushed the horses hard up the arroyo. He was just a boy of twelve winters, but he was nearly a man. Three times already he had ridden with a war party. From the safety of giant yuccas, he had watched braves raid ranches on both sides of the border. Now he was on his fourth and most important war journey. If he proved himself worthy, the tribal council would finally accept him as a full-fledged warrior.

No Chisos Apache boy could wish for more.

Still, Child-of-the-Waters was troubled as he ran the horses into camp a half-mile up the gulch. The seven warriors who waited were not content with stealing horses this time. They were after *pesh-litzogue*—gold. With it, they hoped to buy rifles from the traders in New Mexico. Alchesay, the band's leader, believed it was the only way the Chisos Apaches could become a great people again.

But Child-of-the-Waters wasn't so sure. Orphaned from birth, Child-of-the-Waters had learned at the feet of Oro, the *izze-nantan*, or medicine man. Oro had told him that the mine was cursed. There were ghosts there, and spirits who were angry. They had never forgiven the Chisos Apaches for doing evil against a place that was the very cradle of life.

They had been slaves, but they had chosen to work the mine rather than die with honor. Their sin had brought terrible judgment upon their people. For ninety-two winters the tribe had fallen prey to disease and the white man's firepower. Now only twenty-five families remained of a once-plentiful clan.

The band was dying, and it would never rise again until the mountains' bloody flow was stopped. Child-of-the-Waters had heard Oro himself say it.

Six warriors rushed out to hold the horses, but Alchesay came running up to the youth. Alchesay was the kind of warrior every Chisos Apache boy wanted to be. His eyes were clear and proud, and he wore his thirteen battle wounds like badges of honor. There were scars on his thick chest and below his breechcloth. They covered his hand and arm and marked his nose and cheek. He always seemed to sneer, thanks to another wound that made the corner of his mouth droop.

Like the other braves, Alchesay was outfitted for battle. He wore a war cap of wolf skin, with the tail falling down to the painted shield at his back. Two hanging feathers from an eagle gave his headdress spiritual power. His quiver was filled with hardwood arrows, and he carried a sotol-stalk lance with a gleaming metal point. At Alchesay's hip was a stone-headed war club and a rawhide sheath that bulged with a knife. A well-worn strip of buckskin above his hand told of the many *kahs* or arrows he had let fly. A twanging bowstring always scraped a warrior's wrist.

"Why do you run the horses like *ka-chu*, the jackrabbit?" Alchesay demanded.

Child-of-the-Waters was glad that Alchesay had asked. A novice warrior could speak only if questioned or given permission.

"*Pindah-lickoyee!*" he exclaimed. "White eyes!"

"Where?"

The youth wanted to whirl and point. But it was bad luck for a novice to spin quickly. So Child-of-the-Waters briefly faced *Chigo-na-ay*, the sun, before he turned and slung a hand down the arroyo.

"Halfway to the river! A young *pindah-lickoyee* saw Child-of-the-Waters! He'll tell the two boys that our people the

Shis-Inday are here! I rode like *ittindi* the lightning to tell
Alchesay!"

Alchesay breathed sharply and turned away, wagging his
head in displeasure. It made Child-of-the-Waters feel less like a
warrior than ever. A novice had to learn stealth on the war trail,
and Child-of-the-Waters had failed.

Still, Alchesay held his tongue. Apaches believed that spirit
forces lived in every novice, shaping him the way they wanted.
No matter the offense, a wise man like Alchesay showed a beginning warrior respect. Even Alchesay was afraid of angering the
spirits—except, perhaps, to gain the yellow metal.

Suddenly a war cry echoed through the arroyo, bringing
Alchesay whirling. Child-of-the-Waters quickly scanned the
lofty rim. A squat Apache rider with shining black hair was pulling rein on a black horse. He was looking down on camp and
waving a painted lance against the sky.

"The *pindah-lickoyee* boys ride hard for the river!" cried the
warrior. "Another one follows in their dust! I, Loco, saw them
with my own eyes! We must chase them down! I'll stake them to
an ant bed myself! When the ants crawl, they'll tell us where
pesh-litzogue the yellow iron is!"

A roar of agreement rose from camp. But Alchesay quieted
the warriors with a sweep of his arm.

"Loco thinks like *yah-tats-an*, a dead animal!" he cried. "Are
the rest of you as foolish? All of you know that Oro the *izze-nantan*
wouldn't tell us his secret! He didn't want us to have the yellow
iron to buy rifles with! So he rode away from our lodges and we
followed! We hoped he'd lead us to the yellow iron! He said the
mountains were bleeding at the place of the yellow rock! He said
he needed to heal their wound and appease the vengeful spirits
before he died! We thought he might be headed there!

"We saw Oro point out the Chisos to the young white eyes
just before the Great Spirit *Usen* took him! Oro might have sent
them to do what he couldn't! You yourselves saw the

pindah-lickoyee boy speak with him in the language without words!

"Even now, the boys might have the yellow-iron fever! The *pindah-lickoyee*, even the children, love the yellow rock better than their own lives! The fever will burn hotter and hotter until the boys hold the rock in their hands!"

"Then I'll torture them till they tell us!" shouted Loco.

"Will you always think like a dead animal, Loco?" demanded Alchesay. "Oro was a mighty medicine man! His power was great! If he told the white eyes his secret and we harm them, his ghost will be angry! Why do you think nobody tried to torture the secret out of Oro himself?"

"So what do we do?" demanded Loco.

Alchesay glanced at Child-of-the-Waters.

"The third white eyes has seen us, but we can't let them see us anymore! If they don't feel threatened and they know Oro's secret, they'll start for the yellow iron! They'll lead us there, and we can be a great people again!"

Eight fierce war-whoops rose up around Child-of-the-Waters. But the budding warrior only hung his head and remembered the troubling things that Oro had whispered to him.

CHAPTER 6

· •) ≈ (• ·

F ish didn't know how long he could last.

He clung at arm's length to a half-submerged branch as tons of water rushed into his face. His legs were straight out, caught in the violent flow. He went under and came up and went under again. He was a bobbing cork. He was a toy in the hands of a force mighty enough to carve canyons.

It was too much! He couldn't breathe! He couldn't pull himself out against a current that wouldn't give an inch!

In a detached sort of way, he knew when the cowboy came sweeping downstream. The tumbling figure was headed straight for him, somebody else as helpless as he was. The froth was thick and everything was hard to make out. But Fish thought he could see his would-be rescuer reach for a hanging limb just upstream. Then Fish went under again, and that was the last he saw of him.

Fish kept up his struggle for longer than he would have believed possible. He was tired and weak and his hopes of pulling himself higher were all but dead. It was time to take his chances downstream. He was drowning here!

He was just about to let go when he heard a familiar voice.

"I swan, Fish, if you don't look like a big catfish a-floppin' out there!"

Fish popped up long enough to see a grinning figure in soaked clothes on a sturdy limb almost overhead. When their gazes met, the rawboned teen-ager in the tree grinned even wider.

"Sure makes me wish for my fishin' pole!" the big kid added with a chuckle.

It was Punk! Fun-loving Punk, perched on that limb like a leprechaun!

"Get me outa here!" Fish hollered, just before going under again.

When he came back up, he found a hand drawing near. But Punk was in no hurry. Just before his skinny fingers were in Fish's reach, the impish teen-ager drew back a bit.

"Say," said Punk with a snicker, "maybe you ain't had time for a good bath yet."

"Grab me! Grab me!"

"A feller sure needs a good bath ever' now and then."

"Get me outa here! I mean it, you rascal!"

"Well, why didn't you say so? Give ol' Punk your hand and I'll fish you out. I ain't got all day."

It wasn't easy, but with Punk tugging, Fish managed to fight his way up to safety. Still, the water continued to surge between the willow and dry land. He was lucky enough to find his hat snagged on a broken limb below. About the time he retrieved it, Gid showed up on horseback at water's edge. He threw them a loop and soon they were safely on shore.

Fish was peeved. Punk had sure taken his sweet time back there. But it was hard to fuss at somebody who had just pulled him out of harm's way. Besides, Punk was too fleet of tongue to give him much of a chance.

"You fellers look like a couple of drownded rats," joked the wrangler as he looked them over.

Gid looked dumbfounded. "Where the dickens you come from, Punk?"

"My ma and pa, I reckon. Unless they put in an order with ol' Santy Claus."

Gid went on. "I swum my horse across and went to lookin' for Fish and there *you* was!"

"Yeah, well, ever'body's gotta be somewhere. Even yay-hoos like you two."

Fish was no less amazed. "Boy, Punk, did you ever show up in the nick of time! I seen somebody rope my horse, but I didn't have no idea it was—hey! That was you we was runnin' from, wasn't it! You near got me killed!"

"We thought you was a wild Indian!" exclaimed Gid.

Punk looked back at the river. Suddenly his dimpled features weren't so playful anymore. In all the excitement, he had almost forgotten the Apache.

"Speakin' of Indians . . . ," Punk muttered as he scanned the far bank.

Fish turned with him. He had never heard such a somber tone in Punk's voice. He didn't know what to make of it. But it sure made the hair rise on his scalp.

"What, Punk?" he pressed, looking for he-didn't-know-what. "Speakin' of Indians, *what?*"

Gid's eyes were fixed just as intently on the Mexico bank. "What's the matter, Punk? You gotta tell us!"

Except for yucca and desert shrubs, the Mexico side of the river was clear for now. But Punk's mind was suddenly filled with all kinds of ideas. As long as the river stayed on a rise, no Apache was likely to cross and give them trouble. Punk figured he had plenty of time to hooraw the boys a bit.

"Well, fellers," he said in his most serious voice, "it was likin' to this." He faced them so that he could enjoy their expressions. "Fifty of them savages jumped me way deep in Mexico last night. I whipped out my six-shooter and made that ol' thing go to barkin'. I kept a-firin' and reloadin' and firin' some more, till it got too hot to hold. 'Fore I was finished, I had them thinkin' they was up against General Lee hisself and the whole Rebel army.

"I put them redskins to flight and then I started ridin' for Texas. I kept my ol' pony in a run all night long. Say, looka there, will you? Must've lost my six-shooter in the river. Anyhow, I figure they know better than to tangle with ol' Punk anymore."

Fish and Gid were just as wide-eyed as Punk had hoped. Fish reckoned Punk for as good an Indian fighter as he was a roper. And to hear Punk tell it, he was the best roper in all of Texas and half of Mexico.

"Gee, Punk," he said. "You're awful brave."

"I'll say," agreed Gid. "You think you could ever teach us to shoot thataway?"

"Whew! I ain't sure," said the wrangler with a shake of his head. "You know what they say—some fellers are born with it, and some develop it. Then there's yay-hoos like y'all that are just full of it.

"Anyhow, when we get back to headquarters—say, y'all's mama is mighty worried about you two. When you didn't come back in on time, she sent me a-lookin'. Been trailin' y'all for a couple of days now. What in Sam Hill you up to, anyhow?"

"We're lookin' for a gold mine!" Gid announced proudly.

Punk just looked at him and began to grin as only Punk could."Really, Punk," spoke up Fish. "I know right where it is."

But Punk wasn't convinced. He had an annoying way of always making fun of their every act. His grin became a chuckle that turned into a howling laugh. He laughed so long and hard that Fish figured his sides were bound to ache.

"What's so funny?" asked Gid.

"Yeah, Punk, how come you're always laughin' at us?" chimed in Fish.

"Why, you boys couldn't find your own grandma if she was a-rockin' right under your noses!" roared Punk.

"Yeah, we could!" argued Gid.

"Sure, Punk!" agreed Fish. "You ain't got no idea the things I heard!"

Punk flashed his buckteeth. "Well, now, maybe I *was* a little hasty. I reckon you boys might hear an ol' cat squall, all right. Guess there's always a chance ol' tom could get his tail caught under Grandma's rocker."

The three of them went downstream, looking for the two missing horses. As they searched, Fish and Gid told Punk all about Oro. They described the old fort and the first rays of sunlight striking the Chisos. Fish even told him about the tunnel that was supposed to lead from the mud walls to the Rio Grande. But Punk seemed more interested in poking fun than in hearing what they had to say.

Meanwhile, a change was coming over Fish. The more the wrangler teased him, the more it seemed as if Punk had taken him by the shoulders. In his own way, Punk was shaking some sense into him. By the time they rounded a sweeping bend, Fish was filled with all sorts of doubt. Soon he was asking himself questions.

What was the matter with him, going off on a wild goose chase this way? A gold mine! Why, the very idea! They might as well try to rope the wind! And anyway, what right did he have to chase after something he hadn't earned? Hadn't his pa always taught him the value of hard work? Didn't the Good Book say a person was supposed to sweat for his every bite?

On the Texas bank around another large bend, they found the horses safe and sound. Fish's bay was dragging the frayed rope. Luckily, the lariat had snapped, allowing the animals to untangle and scramble out.

Fish was facing the river as he adjusted his bay's bridle for the ride to the Chisos. With each passing second, he realized more and more his foolishness. He checked the bit in the horse's mouth and looked at the river with a sigh of disgust. It was time to turn these old ponies around and head back to Ma.

Suddenly he saw something that made him change his mind all over again.

"Look!" he cried, pointing across his horse's nose to the high bank across in Mexico.

Under the rim, the foamy waters splashed against the gaping mouth of a mysterious black hole.

It was a tunnel! A shaft ending right at the river and pointing the way to the Chisos, just like Oro had said!

CHAPTER 7

· ⟩ ≋ ⟨ ·

Fish felt like a lost, lonely figure in a sea of strange threat.

He rode with Gid and Punk across a sweeping flat that stretched toward a camel's-hump mountain a few miles away. The lone ridge stood against the higher Chisos, purple and mighty in the distance. There was a sudden drop-off a few hundred yards to his left, and in the depths sprawled a maze of gullies with oddly eroded buttes.

Fish couldn't figure out why he was so anxious, despite what Oro had warned. After all, the sky was blue, the sun was bright, and he could see a lot of peaceful miles in every direction.

Still, even the ordinary seemed spooky on this morning.

There was the wind, moaning like a wandering ghost. There were the spindly stems of many-branched ocotillo, stirring like living skeletons. There were the big sky and sprawling desert, never letting him forget how small and weak he really was.

But there were also Oro's troubling sign words, vivid in his memory.

Fish wanted to run and hide.

He was in the open here, on full display for all those Indian spirits to see. They were angry, and they would stay angry as long as the mountains' wound went unhealed. Here on the trail to the lost mine, the spirits might take the form of animals at any time and threaten him. At least that's what Oro had said.

Fish was glad he wasn't Apache. If he had been, he might have believed all of that. Still, the desert creatures gave him plenty of reason to think twice about the matter.

There was the unseen wolf, howling as if the midday sun were really the moon. There was the hidden owl, hooting as if the glare of day were really the black of night. There were the scorpions and pack rats, more creatures of the evening that suddenly favored light.

Maybe things weren't so ordinary after all, thought Fish. It was as if every creature of the night had been turned loose upon the day.

Still, Fish was a cowboy, just like his father had been. And a cowboy didn't have any business hightailing it from some silly Indian legend.

"I never seen so many spiders and things crawlin'," said Gid, leaning over the side of his horse for a better look. "Don't that mean it's supposed to rain or somethin', Punk?"

"Yeah, Punk, what's it mean?" asked Fish. He was hoping for any answer that didn't involve Apache spirits.

Around these innocent-faced boys, Punk was never one to admit to a lack of knowledge. Why should he, when he could make them believe just about anything he wanted? After all, they were young, trusting, and plenty "green," as an older cowboy would say. That meant they still had a lot to learn.

His eyes twinkled as he looked the boys over. "I declare, fellers. Ol' Adam hisself could've took lessons from y'all."

"What do you mean?" asked Fish.

Punk's grin widened. "Keepin' up that garden of his. You know—Eden."

"Huh?" said Gid.

Punk fought back a snicker. "They say you sure can grow stuff if you got a green thumb. And seein' how you two's green as gourds from head to toe, I reckon y'all could make corn sprout out of a chicken's back. Don't y'all know that spiders a-crawlin' in daytime means—

"Say, listen to that eagle, will you?"

Sure enough, from somewhere behind came the cry of an eagle. Fish turned in the saddle and checked the sky. All he could see was the glaring sun. But now he heard a sound he couldn't identify. It was a quiet rush of air, but it had nothing to do with the wind.

The *whoosh* grew louder. Suddenly something blotted out the sun. At the same instant, Fish realized what he was hearing. It was the sound of a bird of prey in a dive!

"Watch out!" warned Gid.

Fish dodged as a sudden silhouette dropped straight toward him. He cried out as sharp talons ripped through his shirt and grazed his shoulder. Then broad wings were flapping fiercely and carrying the bald eagle up into the sky ahead of him.

"Holy smokes!" exclaimed Gid, whirling to his cousin. "That thing went right for you!"

Punk broke out laughing. "If that don't take the cake!" he roared. "Guess that bunch of feathers figured him for a jack rabbit! Come to think of it, them big ears of his *do* kinda look like ol' Hoppity's!"

Fish didn't think it was so funny as he checked his shoulder. His shirt was shredded and his skin was all red. He had been attacked by an eagle!

"Did he draw blood?" asked Gid, bringing his horse closer. "Gosh, wait'll Papa hears this! He won't believe it!"

Fish wouldn't have either, except for—

A sudden chill ran down his spine. Hadn't Oro warned him about this? Wasn't this why the old Indian had never gone back, even though it was the only way to make peace with those spirits?

Punk was still howling with glee. "I swear, Fish! You dropped your head quicker than a chicken's under Grandma's ax! You boys can sure cheer a feller up! Why, y'all could make a dead possum grin like a silly goose! I ain't never—"

While Punk was hoorawing, Fish was scanning the sky. If there really was such a thing as an Indian spook, it might not give up easily.

"—seen the like of it!" Punk went on. "Why, back there in sixty-six—"

"He's comin' back!" exclaimed Fish, pointing over Punk's head. "Look out!"

Punk whirled and saw the eagle swooping down again. But this time it seemed less interested in Fish than it did in somebody else. It was bearing straight for Punk—and suddenly things didn't seem so funny to the wrangler anymore.

"Ride for your lives!" Punk hollered, putting spurs to his sorrel and heading for the drop-off. "He's a-comin' like a cyclone!"

Fish and Gid gigged their horses and took off after him. Fish sure hoped there was shelter down in those badlands. His pony had just reached an all-out gallop when a fast-moving shadow appeared on the ground alongside. The shadow raced on past and suddenly the eagle was straight ahead. It extended its talons for the dodging wrangler and missed by only a hair. Then the raptor was soaring into the sky again and veering back into the sun.

"He near got me!" yelled Punk, slapping a hand to his scalp. "Ride, Punk' ol' boy! Ride like you're late for supper!"

Fish rode so bent over that his cheek almost brushed his horse's neck. He wished he could get even lower. He felt thirty feet tall out here. He was a target ripe for the picking. He could almost feel those talons already digging into his skin. Even a rabbit had a chance to make it to his hole. Where could a twelve-year-old boy go that an eagle couldn't follow?

"Here he comes again!" shouted Gid. "He's right on our tail!"

Fish didn't have to look back to know that Gid was right. He could tell plenty by the growing hiss in the air. How in blue blazes was he going to get out of this! Eagles just didn't act this way! All this talk about gold and spirits and creatures becoming devils—what had he gotten himself into!

Just when Fish thought things couldn't get any worse, Gid sounded a frantic warning. "Dat-gum! He's on you!"

Fish cringed and felt the raptor's talons right through his hat. He cried out and fumbled for a grip as he slid down along the horse's shoulder. He had to get the thing off him!

He felt a rush of wind in his hair and suddenly he was free of both hat and eagle. But he was far from out of the woods. He was off-balance and couldn't find the saddle horn! The flailing hoofs were flying up, and so was the hard-packed ground! He was tumbling right off a running horse, and there was nothing he could do about it!

Suddenly his spur caught in the cinch, the band that ran around his bay's belly and held the saddle in place. He hit the ground bouncing, dragged by a pony in an all-out run.

"He's hung, Punk! He's hung!"

Gid's cry was almost lost to Fish amid the thunder of iron-shod hoofs. They were in his eyes, raising dust and slinging gravel. They were ready to crush his skull, but the surging ground was even more deadly. Already it was peeling the hide off his shoulders. It was punishing him, but something even more sinister lay in wait. Any moment, he might catch a lechuguilla dagger in the face or an eagle claw cactus in the ribs. He might take a rock to the head, or uproot a yucca that didn't want to be uprooted. Any way he looked at it, things were as hopeless as they came.

He knew he had only three chances.

His spur leather could break. Punk or Gid could head off the horse. Or somebody could shoot the clabberhead.

But Punk had lost his revolver, the bay was racing on unchecked, and Fish was sporting new leather on his spurs.

Suddenly he realized that the drop-off was almost upon him. Still, he was helpless to do anything but cry out and say a quick prayer. At the last moment, the charging horse made a sharp cut to avoid going over. The force slung Fish toward the rim, and the change in angle tore his spur from the cinch.

As the horse raced away, momentum drove Fish over a sotol clump and through a last line of prickly pear. He was tumbling crazily, then suddenly the world dropped out from under him.

He was plunging head-over-heels into a canyon!

CHAPTER 8

· • ⟩ ∿ ⟨ • ·

Even as Alchesay instructed him in the ways of the desert, Child-of-the-Waters worried about all the angry spirits.

The novice and the war chief rode at the back of the war party across a sprawling flat. Past the camel's-hump mountain ahead, the hazy crags of the Chisos grew ever higher. For several miles Alchesay had pointed the way, leaning over his paint horse to trace the white boys' path. Then the war chief had dropped back alongside Child-of-the-Waters and left the tracking to Loco.

They were in Texas now, but crossing over from Mexico hadn't been easy. Child-of-the-Waters had never seen the river spirits so angry. For three hours he and the full-fledged warriors had waited for the Rio Grande to go down. Even then, the waters had been so swift that the young Apache had thought twice before plunging his horse off the bank.

He had clung desperately to his swimming animal all the way across. It had been awfully scary, but a novice had to show courage above all else. Still, if he hadn't gritted his teeth, his jaw surely would have trembled.

Now he worried that the desert spirits might be even more displeased than those in the Rio Grande. All the way from its banks, a wolf had howled in the distance. An owl was calling too. And just minutes ago the ground had come alive with scorpions and spiders.

Maybe Oro had been right.

Maybe the Chisos Mountains still bled from a century-old wound. Maybe the spirits were showing their anger by unleashing creatures of the night into the day. Maybe the spirit animals would even rise up and threaten them as they went farther down this trail to the yellow iron.

"You're riding next to me, but you seem as far away as *yandestan* the sky."

The irritation in Alchesay's voice shook Child-of-the-Waters from his fog.

"Yes, Alchesay?" the boy asked, quickly looking up.

There was impatience in the war chief's features. "The desert can kill, or it can save," the man said sternly. "But a warrior who doesn't listen is already dead."

Child-of-the-Waters swallowed hard. He knew that he was expected to learn a warrior's survival skills by journey's end. But as he glanced down in shame, he saw the spiders and scorpions all the more clearly.

The war chief scanned the badlands and swept a hand from horizon to horizon. "See the desert? See how great it is? It chokes the life from all but the strongest. But a warrior's greatest strength is in his thoughts."

Child-of-the-Waters frowned. How could a man's thoughts bend a bow or hurl a lance? Or carry him across a scorching desert such as this? He wanted to ask, but a novice was not permitted.

"Your face holds many questions," observed Alchesay. "It asks, 'If I grow weak under *Chigo-na-ay* the sun, how can my thoughts keep me alive?'"

Alchesay patted his war pony on the neck before continuing. "I'll tell you something every *Shis-Inday* should know. You can walk far without a horse. You can fight without a bow. You can watch the moons come and go as your stomach stays empty. But there's one thing that no warrior can do without."

"Water?" suggested the youth, eager to make up for his earlier inattention.

The war chief took hold of a bag that dangled from his shoulder by a rawhide loop. Child-of-the-Waters had one too. It was a water pouch made from coyote intestine.

"I'll tell you a secret," said Alchesay, shaking the contents a little. "It's not thirst that kills quickly. It's the fear in knowing you're thirsty. It's the same with everything. Fear is the enemy."

The war chief bent over the side of his horse and scooped up a few pebbles from the ground. He straightened and held them out in an open palm.

"Take some on your tongue," said Alchesay.

The youth did as he was told.

"Now roll them around in your mouth," instructed the war chief. "See how it waters? Your body might thirst, but your mind won't. Chase away the fear and maybe you'll stay alive to taste real water."

Indeed, Child-of-the-Water's mouth was moist. Still, he couldn't keep from studying the forbidding desert. As far as he could see, there was nothing but cacti and creosote and barren crags baked by a killer sun.

"I see more questions in your face," observed Alchesay. "Ask them if you like."

"The river's far behind us now," said the boy. "Where could a warrior find water where there's only sun and dirt?"

The war chief called the boy's attention to the ground by dropping the remaining pebbles. "Even if the ground is dry, water can sleep under it. Remember the cottonwoods in the dry arroyos, and the stained cliffs where desert meets mountain. Dig where there's reason to, and the Great Spirit *Usen* might give you what you look for. You have more questions, Child-of-the-Waters?"

"Yes."

"Ask me."

"If it's not water that a warrior can't do without, what is it?"

"Courage," replied Alchesay.

Suddenly the war chief seemed to pierce him through and through, and Child-of-the-Waters was sorry he had asked. He realized now that Alchesay knew that he was just a scared little boy. There could be no harsher judgment on a novice, and he hung his head in disgrace.

"Child-of-the-Waters," said Alchesay.

"Yes?" whispered the youth.

"Look at me, Child-of-the-Waters."

The novice lifted his gaze to find unusual concern in the war chief's face.

"What troubles you so much?" asked Alchesay. "Why is there such worry in your eyes since we left the river?"

Child-of-the-Waters glanced at all the creeping things on the ground. "We're riding the trail to the yellow iron and the spirits are angry with us. They've taken the form of spiders and scorpions, and soon they'll send terrible spirit creatures swooping down."

"Who said so?"

"Oro the *Izze-nantan*."

Child-of-the-Waters had never seen Alchesay go so pale before. His face became almost ashen. The war chief's gaze dropped to the tarantula at his horse's hoofs, and he seemed stunned into silence. All he could do was look with awe upon first one crawling thing, then another. Finally he lifted his eyes and started to speak. But the words died in Loco's quick cry of alarm.

Child-of-the-Waters looked to the sun for its blessing and then whirled. The war party ahead was splitting. Four warriors wheeled their horses to the left, the rest to the right. As a break formed down the middle, Child-of-the-Waters saw a bobcat bolting out of a shrubby tarbush thirty steps ahead.

It was the largest cat of its kind that the young warrior had ever seen. It was fully four feet long from stubby tail to erect ears. Its forelegs were thick and muscled, and its paws bulged with retractable claws that could seize an animal many times its size. The cat was shaking its head oddly, slinging foam from its mouth to the dark markings on its yellow-white coat.

Child-of-the-Waters knew that bobcats usually feared man and avoided him. But he could read terrible menace in this one's glaring eyes. They burned with the fever madness that white men called rabies.

Maybe that's why the wildcat didn't turn and run. Maybe that's why it bared its sharp fangs and uttered a piercing scream. Maybe that's why it suddenly sprang toward Loco's horse.

Maybe.

But Child-of-the-Waters knew differently. He had heard Oro's warning for himself.

With an oath, Loco prodded his horse away, barely eluding a swipe of the bobcat's claws. The cat spun and gave another squall that chilled Child-of-the-Waters to the bone. Alchesay was the first to nock an arrow and let it fly. At the bowstring's twang, the bobcat jumped—just enough for the arrow to sail by harmlessly.

More warriors lifted their bows, but the cat was as elusive as the wind. It made a run at a second rider, then a third, as arrow after arrow thudded into the ground. A fourth warrior reined his horse out of harm's way, and suddenly Child-of-the-Waters was face-to-face with a charging bobcat.

Over his horse's ears, he could see more than he wanted to in those brief seconds.

He could see the froth flecking its crazed face and the green eyes burning hotter than ever with the fever madness. He could see a predator's teeth anxious to bite and half-hidden claws eager to tear. But worst of all, he seemed to be able to peer behind the animal mask and see the thing for what it really was.

It was a brood of spirits, angry for a century-old sin against the mountains.

Child-of-the-Waters fitted a blunt arrow to his bow even as the details flooded him. Bending a bow was almost second nature to him by now. By his fifth winter, Oro had given him his first small weapon. By his seventh winter, he was felling sparrows from trees. Not two moons ago, he had brought down a twelve-point buck in the del Carmens. But this was a life-or-death matter, and he hadn't learned yet to control his fear.

He took quick aim over his horse's head and unleashed the arrow in sheer panic.

He did only one thing wrong. He forgot to allow for the pony's left ear.

The feathered shaft clipped it and veered off-target. The startled horse went wild. It downed its head and suddenly Child-of-the-Waters was astride a tornado. Caught unawares, he could only grasp at air as the horse kicked toward *Chigo-na-ay* the sun. The next thing he knew, he was tumbling helplessly down the animal's shoulder.

He struck the ground hard at the thrashing hoofs. Whirling, he saw the rabid bobcat almost upon him. There were vengeful spirits behind every claw and fang. There were a thousand more in its eerie eyes. It was a devil cat, leaping straight for his throat, and there was nothing he could do to stop it!

CHAPTER 9

· •) ≈ (• ·

Fish was like a runaway wagon wheel.

He struck the steep slope of the canyon in a frenzied roll. With every turn he built up speed. The sky was above, below, to the side. It traded places with the blurry ground at a dizzying rate. By the time he was halfway down, sky and dirt blended until he couldn't tell the two apart. The sun was a blinding orb that seemed to hang against the gulch bottom.

It was the wildest of wild rides. All he could do was try to control his descent with slapping arms and flailing legs. If he got out of this without a broken neck, he would have some powerful thanking to do.

Suddenly there were distant javelinas in his spinning world. They were racing through the sky and skipping across the canyon floor. There were a dozen of these wild pigs with salt-and-pepper coats, and they were getting closer by the instant. They were grunting and turning their snouts toward him, and Fish sure wasn't anxious to tangle with them. If those teeth of theirs could shred prickly pear and lechuguilla, they might be able to rip open a leg just as easily.

Even as he rolled off a final shelf, he knew he was headed for a showdown.

He dropped the last few spinning feet to the bare wash but never hit it. Suddenly there was coarse, bristly hair cushioning his fall. There was the squeal of a startled pig and his own shriek of alarm. He had landed smack-dab on top of a javelina!

He didn't know a boar could grow so large. But he had never seen one from this angle before. From wiggly tail to hairless snout, it was almost as long as he was tall. If he outweighed this barrel-bellied critter with the stubby legs, it wasn't by much.

Fish did some fast thinking.

If eagles on this trail would attack people for no cause, what about javelinas that had every right to be mad? Wouldn't they be right in the middle of him as soon as he hit the ground? Wouldn't they go to cutting and slashing? Jumping Jehoshaphat! He might never get on his feet, much less get away!

He seized the javelina by its ears and held on for dear life. At least this way he wouldn't be quite so helpless if the beady-eyed devils rushed him.

He had never figured a javelina to be so powerful. With a loud snort, the animal bolted. Suddenly he was being dragged down the gulch, his boots carving trails in the loose dirt behind him.

Fish had ridden his share of pitching broncs and kicking mules. On the Pecos trail, he had even taken a seat on a saddle towed by a wild longhorn. But he had never straddled a beast that could churn its legs like this one could. It was a regular whirlwind, the way it hurtled down the eroded wash.

Suddenly all the javelinas were running with him. They were grunting and snorting and kicking up dust. Their eyes had a

glassy look, as if they were in a trance. Somehow they reminded
Fish of a Bible story his father had read him. There had been a
man possessed by devils, and Jesus had cast them into a herd of
pigs. The animals had gone mad and stampeded right over a—
    "Cliff!"
    The moment he cried out, he was no longer just seeing the
story in his mind's eye; he was living it. Just yards ahead, the
whole canyon floor suddenly dropped out of sight. It was a
pour-off, falling God-only-knew how far straight down! The wild
pigs were headed straight over it, just like in the Good Book! The
javelinas were about to plunge to their deaths, and they were taking him with them!
    He let go of the boar's ears and rolled from its back. He low-
ered his shoulder to catch the ground and somersaulted with a cry
toward the cliff. He came up out of his tumble at the very brink,
but he couldn't stop his forward motion. He was headed straight
for a long, long sleep from which he wouldn't ever wake up.
    Even as he twisted around and clawed at the rock, the
javelinas were rushing by him on either side. They were plummeting headlong over the rim, and his legs were going with them.
    His fingers slashed quick trails through the rubble, and sud-
denly there was no longer rock beneath him. The cliff side was
shooting up before his face! The sky was disappearing, and a hundred feet straight down, his grave was waiting!
    Suddenly his boots were crashing through thorny branches
that popped and splintered. It was a twisted mesquite, jutting out
of the sheer cliff to cling fragilely between earth and sky. Down
through its interlocked limbs he could see a deadly jumble of
boulders far below.
    Pa! he cried silently, scratching at the surging wall. Some-
body help me, Pa!
    Faced with sure death, Fish guessed it was only fitting that he
call on somebody who had already been through it.

He slammed hard into the mesquite and clawed for a hold. The tree creaked mightily as rubble exploded from its base. It threatened to give way entirely, but it had just enough spring to absorb the impact. The next thing Fish knew, he was lodged and swinging up and down with its limbs. He was snagged, while rocks and broken branches hurtled on toward the boulders!

But his troubles were far from over. The rim was out of reach, and spells of run-off had worn the cliff face smooth of handholds. He was trapped! He couldn't climb up, and he couldn't climb down! He was going to hang here until he died!

· •) ≋ (• ·

As the rabid bobcat leaped for Child-of-the-Waters, an arrow whirred in flight. The wicked point caught the vicious animal in midair, impeding its spring. The devils were already fleeing its eyes by the time it hit the ground, a mere hand's width short of the boy.

The wildcat squirmed for an instant, and then it was dead. But Child-of-the-Waters had plenty of life left. He rolled away with a cry and looked up to see Alchesay lowering his bow.

The novice warrior was trembling, but Alchesay didn't notice. The war chief was too busy staring with awe at the devil cat he had felled with a feathered shaft. Alchesay was a fearless warrior in battle, but he was ashen right now. Even a war chief hesitated to stand against angry spirits.

Loco brought his horse closer and drew rein over the dead animal.

"It had the fever madness," he said, studying the foam about its bared fangs.

Child-of-the-Waters thought he could see Alchesay shudder.

"No," said the war chief, holding his stare at the wildcat. "It had the madness of devils."

With a start, Loco pulled his snorting horse back. He wasn't the only warrior to wheel his mount and check his flank.

"Oro had powerful medicine—we've angered his ghost!" someone shouted.

"Not Oro," corrected Alchesay, "but the vengeful spirits he spoke of."

His words were calm, but they sent a chill through Child-of-the-Waters. He wasn't alone in his panic.

"If they send one devil animal, they'll send more!" exclaimed a warrior.

"What do we do?" cried Loco, spinning his horse back to the war chief. He brandished his bow and a handful of arrows. "What good are these if blood doesn't flow through their veins?"

Child-of-the-Waters knew that Alchesay had always respected the spirit world and the evil it could bring an Apache. But the war chief's desire for gold and rifles must have been greater than his fear.

Alchesay slung a hand toward the lifeless beast. "Look!" he cried. "See my arrow? See how it brought down the devil cat? If the spirit animals fall to just one arrow, their medicine's weak! Our arrows are stronger than fangs and claws! We are *Shis-Inday*—Apaches! Nothing can hurt a *Shis-Inday* but his own fear!"

Child-of-the-Waters wasn't so sure, but Alchesay's confident cry led even him to take heart again. Meanwhile, a wave of boldness swept through the war party.

"Even devils fall before our arrows!" cried Loco, bending his bow and sinking another shaft in the carcass.

"Even devils!" cried another, waving his war lance.

Suddenly every warrior was taking up the cry and brandishing a weapon. Even Child-of-the-Waters was caught up in the excitement, and Alchesay seized the moment.

"Ride!" he shouted, lifting his bow against the hazy Chisos. "Ride for *Pesh-litzogue*, the yellow iron!"

And as Child-of-the-Waters sprang to his feet and ran for his horse, Oro's warning suddenly seemed long ago and foolish.

CHAPTER 10

· •) ≋ (• ·

On the face of a sheer cliff, Fish dangled from a gnarled limb that suddenly groaned.

It dropped a few inches, and stark terror seized him. He couldn't breathe. His heart began drumming wildly. He kicked at the cliff, searching for a hold that wasn't there. Rubble flew from the mesquite's base and plunged to the depths. He could feel the limb giving, little by little, threatening to send him to his death.

Near the mossy wall the tree forked, sending a twisted branch skyward. It looked to be sturdy, but it hovered out of reach. Fish had just begun fighting for it through a tangle of thorns when he shied at a sudden sound. With a piercing *craaack!* louder than any rifle shot, the supporting limb burst at the fork.

Suddenly he was swinging, dropping! The stress was splitting the mesquite all the way to its knobby root! He still had a grip, but the breaking limb was carrying him down with it!

With a cry, Fish slammed into the cliff. The crushing blow rattled his senses and knocked the wind out of him. But somehow he held on, dangling half-stunned with the suspended limb over a deadly gorge.

He looked up with a moan as splintered twigs rained down. The fractured limb hugged the cliff all the way up to the split mesquite. The upper branches were still there, clawing against the sky. But his own limb hung from the base by a mere finger of wood and bark.

The firm branches were so close overhead but so impossibly far. And Fish suddenly was so dazed, so impossibly weak.

It was like a dream. Or a nightmare. One that was taking him straight to an early grave.

He hung his head as he began to slip, and suddenly his dead father seemed very, very close. He was there beside him, urging him to cling to that dangling limb. His pa was telling him not to give up, that he still had plenty of trails to ride. He was begging him to—

Something struck Fish on the shoulder. A branch maybe, or a fair-sized rock. Whatever it was, it seemed to lie there against his chest and fall down his legs. There was something odd about the thing, the way it ended below his squirming boots and curved up, looping the air.

Then something began to pierce his fog, a little at a time. It was a frantic voice, calling out of the sky, spiraling down out of a great funnel that went on forever.

"Fish! Fish! You hear me, Fish? Listen to me!"

There was another voice too, a deeper one with an unmistakable Texas drawl.

"Latch on to that rope, Fish ol' boy! Grab a-hold good and let ol' Punk reel you in like a pollywog!"

"You gotta put that loop around you!" urged the first voice. "You gotta catch a-hold! You gotta do it, Fish! You just gotta!"

Fish was still in a daze. But when he found the loop rising along his rib cage, he slipped his head and one arm through.

"Now hold on, ol' feller!" shouted the deeper voice. "This ol' horse is gonna back you outa there like you's a ol' cow bogged in the mud!"

The words no sooner had funneled down to Fish than the suspended limb ripped free above him. He was too addled even to be afraid as he plummeted with it. Suddenly the loop was tightening around him, burning his shoulder and back. An instant later it jerked taut, and he was like a hanged man dangling there with his boot heels clicking together.

"Get him up before he strangles, Punk!" a voice exclaimed.

"Aw, now, don't go a-frettin' so," said the other. "You think ol' Punk would let a feller down? I'll have him up 'fore you can say 'my horse has fleas!'"

· •) ≋ (• ·

It looked like a place of awful judgment.

Fish didn't get clear-headed until they rode into a gap between the camel's hump mountain and a ridge. It almost made him wish he were still in a daze. If he had been, he wouldn't have felt such a sudden chill.

He found the crowding bluffs hanging over him, twin jumbles of dark, volcanic boulders ready to roll down and crush. He had never seen a place so ghastly. Not even a cactus clung to the slopes. It was a moonscape, rooted in some long-ago upheaval that had laid waste to it.

The gap pointed the way to the Chisos, all right. But right now it looked more like the gate to hell.

"Can't be over ten miles on to them mountains," offered Gid as their horses picked their way through scattered boulders. "They's sure mighty rough-lookin'. Least, it ought to be cooler sleepin' than it was back in them mud walls."

Fish drew rein behind the youths and stared at those hazy Chisos spires. They seemed to rise up so powerful and mysterious, even haunted. "I . . . I ain't so sure we oughta spend the night up there," he said with a shudder.

Punk pulled rein on his sorrel and looked around at him with a grin. "You finally come alive back there, Fish ol' boy? For a spell, I thought I was gonna have to tote you across the front of my saddle like a dogie calf."

Gid had held his horse too, and now he was checking Fish's eyes. "You gettin' your wits back some? Gosh, you've had me plum' worried. How you feelin'?"

"Better than he looks, I hope," spoke up Punk. "I swan, you couldn't prove it by me but what he'd been clawed, throwed, drug, dropped, and hung. Say, ain't that just what happened? I just wish my ol' grandma was here. She sure loves a good laugh. And ol' Fish there could keep her in regular stitches for a month of Sundays."

But Fish was in no mood for jokes. He was still staring at the Chisos, and those misty crags were looking more haunted by the second.

"So why don't you wanna spend the night in them mountains?" Gid asked him. "Ain't that where we gotta go?"

"I reckon," Fish replied quietly. He kept his gaze fast on those peaks. "Gid, why we doin' this anyhow?"

"Doin' what?"

"Chasin' after that gold."

"'Cause that ol' Indian told you 'bout it. Least, that's what you told me."

"I know that. But why is it we're wantin' it?"

"Wouldn't ever'body want a stash of money? Gosh, think of it! Papa ain't hardly had any cash dollars since before the war. You know that. If he comes ridin' in from New Mexico without findin' a buyer for them steers of his, times will be tougher than ever. We're liable to be headin' back to some dusty ol' East Texas farm. You'd be a-tradin' in that cow pony of yours for some stubborn ol' plow mule."

Fish sure didn't want that. After all, he was a cowboy, just like his pa had been. But knowing that didn't make him feel any better right now. He was starting to believe too much in all that Indian superstition. His clawed shoulder, his skinned back, the scratches from that cliff-side mesquite—they wouldn't let him forget it for a second.

"Well, I'll tell you what ol' Punk'd do with any gold you fellers ever led him to," spoke up the wrangler sarcastically. "I'd slap it between two skunks and eat it like a sandwich. Hide, hair, and all."

"You still ain't a-believin' us, Punk?" asked Gid. "Even after seein' that ol' tunnel across the Rio Grande?"

Punk snickered. "All I seen was a mud cave. Oh yeah, and a couple of yay-hoos who'd go chasin' the wind if somebody was to tell 'em they could catch it. I'm just taggin' along 'cause you fellers are more entertainin' than a fryin' pan full of cobbler. Say, wouldn't that taste good with that skunk sandwich right now.... Ummm!"

"Maybe we oughta..." Fish took a deep breath and turned to his companions. "What would y'all think about us...you know, turnin' back?"

"How come?" asked Gid, with all kinds of surprise. "We're just startin' to get close, ain't we?"

"I sure was lookin' forward to havin' me that skunk sandwich," Punk urged in his own way.

"I...." Fish went quiet. The Chisos had seized his eye again.

"So what's wrong all of a sudden?" asked Gid.

"I...I reckon I just ain't hankerin' to go sharin' my bed with a bunch of mad spooks."

"Whaddaya mean, *spooks*?" asked Gid, his eyes wide.

"Spooks. You know—boogers. Ghosts and spirits."

Punk gave a grin that became a snicker that became a roaring laugh. His howl carried to the bluffs and came rolling back, louder than ever. The echoes were mighty creepy, and Fish and Gid gave quick looks around to see if anything was sneaking up.

"Dat-gum, Punk!" exclaimed Fish. "You have to do that? You're gonna make them Indian spirits madder than ever!"

It only made the wrangler laugh harder. But Gid was mighty serious as he turned back to lecture his cousin.

"It's bad enough puttin' up with Punk's hoorawin' all the time without you startin' it too! Papa says all them stories about ghosts in the Chisos is just superstition!"

"I ain't hoorawin'. And I don't think Oro was neither when he told me about them spooks."

"You never said nothin' about no spooks before! I thought we was brothers now! What else ain't you told me? Since when you go to believin' ever'thing some ol' Indian tells you?"

"I reckon if we put any stock in what he had to say about that gold, it'd pay us to listen to whatever else he had to tell. He was sure right about that eagle and them javelinas."

"What about 'em?" Gid pressed with a frown.

"He said the spirits was angry about that ol' mine. He said they'd come after us in the form of animals. He said we'd know we're on the right trail when they did. I...I'm gettin' scared, Gid."

Punk was still howling. But he calmed himself long enough to cock his head to the side and study Fish like a confused dog. "I swan! Look at ol' Fish there, will you? Why, that fall's still got him as addled as a new-borned calf! Doggone, I can't even hooraw him about it good yet! He ain't clear-headed enough to appreciate it! Indian spooks in a bunch of squealin' pigs! Why, smell my ol' toe jam! What's a feller to think?"

Suddenly all the horses shied at once. Fish glanced at the wrangler's sorrel and caught quick movement in the trail just ahead of it. Fish did a double take and found the ground strangely alive. "You tell *me*, Punk!"

"Huh? What?"

Fish slung a hand toward the base of a boulder only yards past the wrangler. "You tell *me* what to think about them rattlers comin' at us!"

"They's all around us!" exclaimed Gid.

Fish whirled. Sure enough, there was a tangle of western diamondbacks closing in on all sides. They formed such a seething mass that he couldn't tell which scaly heads went with which sets of rattles. But there was no mistaking the eyes—cold, evil orbs locked in awful stares. They came flicking their forked tongues, a brood of snakes acting in unheard-of fashion, and the horses were terrified.

"Them rattle-tails is thicker than maggots on a dead cow!" hollered Punk, his grin suddenly gone.

"These horses are liable to go wild!" exclaimed Fish.

"Be still!" urged Punk. "You fellers gotta be still!"

Fish had heard his pa say the same thing: If a person froze, a rattlesnake wouldn't strike. But somebody forgot to inform Fish's horse, for the boogered bay was suddenly rearing with him.

"Easy, boy! Easy!"

Fish was lucky to stay in the saddle as the snorting bay pawed at the sky. When the animal came down, Fish knew they couldn't just wait around to be thrown off in a den of poisonous fangs.

"We gotta ride!" he cried to Punk, who blocked the trail ahead. "Go, Punk, go!"

Desperate times called for desperate measures, and Punk got the message. "You slimy things ain't gonna tickle ol' Punk's toes!" he cried, gigging his horse up-trail toward the advancing rattlers. "Y'all look meaner than ol' Grunt with his mad face on!"

The line of snakes was maybe a yard deep, and Punk's sorrel cleared it easily and was off to the races. Gid followed suit on his roan, and Fish wasn't far behind. As he spurred his bay toward the rattlers, he didn't know which pounded more, the hoofs of his horse or his runaway heart.

"Up, boy!" he cried, urging his animal into a jump at the last instant.

They seemed to hang in air forever. But when they came down, the deadly ring of snakes was behind them.

As the bay chased after the other horses and riders, Fish glanced back. The dust hung over the gap like a shroud. If a fellow went back through there anytime soon, a shroud was exactly what somebody would be covering him with in a freshly dug grave. Ahead, the Chisos suddenly looked closer and more ghostly than ever. It sure wasn't Fish's first choice for a good night's sleep. But Punk and Gid had their horses in a gallop straight for its mightiest canyon, and one thing was sure. Fish didn't intend to be left alone out here with all these prowling spirits.

"Hyaaah!"

He patted his pony on the neck and urged it toward those mountains of mystery.

· •) ≈ (• ·

CHAPTER 11

At the yawning mouth of Juniper Canyon, they rode upon a muddy spring under a five-hundred-foot bluff. Over its rim, Fish could see a much higher wall hanging in the sky. It was a massive upthrust, rising three thousand feet to jagged cliffs that stretched for miles. Fish had heard Papa Guy call it the South Rim.

Northeastward across the broad canyon was another mountain barrier just as imposing. But this wall was even more mysterious. Somewhere beyond was the skyline bump that he had sighted-in from the old mission door. All the way from rattlesnake gap, he had plotted a course to that crown of rock that supposedly marked the old mine. He had lost it now against the heights. But it was stronger than ever in his mind.

Suddenly so much of what Oro had told him just didn't make sense anymore. All that stuff about the cradle of life—who could believe something like that? How could a mineshaft hurt

mountains so mighty? And if in some strange way it had, so
what? What could a twelve-year-old boy do about it? It was true
that Oro had begged him to heal these mountains. But how could
he, when the old Apache hadn't explained how?

Now the walls seemed to tower even higher, reminding Fish
how puny he was and how little he really knew.

Then he posed another silent question to these tight-lipped
crags. If so much gold had been wrenched from them already,
what harm would there be in taking one more saddlebag full?
After all, it could sure pull Papa Guy out of a hole.

Fish was plenty troubled, but one thought weighed heaviest
on his mind. What would his dead father—a man who had
believed in working for everything he got—have said about it all?

He dwelled on the matter as the horses pawed at the spring's
slushy pool and watered. He was getting plenty dry too, and so
were Gid and Punk. But a mud hole like this was no place to dip a
canteen.

Hugging the ever-rising bluff, they trailed up Juniper Canyon
for three or four miles. At first there were only agave, pitaya,
guayacan, and other desert shrubs and cacti. Then the canyon
drainage began to thicken with dark-needled juniper trees. Just
before sundown, they pulled rein where the bluff abruptly gave
way at an arroyo feeding down out of the west. The bluff bent
sharply with the arroyo, forming a wall to a side canyon. Brushy
and winding, the gorge climbed steadily toward the high country's hanging cliffs.

"My backside's sure a-painin' me," groaned Gid. "It'd suit
me fine if we didn't go another step tonight."

"Got decent grazin' here for the horses, all right," noted Fish.

"Yeah, and I see a spot yonder just achin' for my bedroll,"
offered Punk. "Say, you fellers don't figure on stompedin' no cattle through camp tonight, do you? Naw, reckon not—'less that
bunch you boogered last year is still on the run. Anyhow, ol'
Punk's here to look out for you fellers. I'll dig out my tins of grub

if one of you will rustle up some firewood and the other one will mosey up this side-canyon lookin' for water. Appears to be a spring up thataway, from all the growth."

Fish wasn't anxious to go wandering off alone in these spooky crags. But he and Gid flipped an old Rebel coin and Fish lost. He resisted even then, but finally he gave in. He was a cowboy, and no cowboy could be a coward. With three canteens dangling from his neck, he nervously pushed out on foot up through the junipers.

Little did he know that at that very moment another boy afoot was dropping down into the side-canyon from the hovering bluff. It was an Apache youth, and over his shoulder were the straps of nine pouches fashioned from coyote intestine. The warriors were thirsty, and it was a novice's job to get water.

The war party had trailed the young whites all the way to the mud hole at the canyon mouth. There, the warriors had taken to the high ground, tracing a torturous path up the bluff and along its rim to avoid being seen. Even now, seven warriors were making camp on a flat far above Child-of-the-Waters. The eighth, Loco, had taken bow in hand and set off in search of game.

As the *Shis-Inday* youth slid down the steep slope, he dwelled on all that Oro had told him in secret about these mountains. After the Great Spirit *Usen* had made the world, he had scattered the leftover rocks here and called it Chisos. On that day, the earth had shook, rumbled, and moaned. All life, even their people the *Shis-Inday*, had begun in the Chisos. When the last of the *Shis-Inday* died, the world would come to an end.

That dark hour, Oro had warned, was drawing near. And it was the Apaches' own fault. They had helped open a wound that even now was draining the blood from the very cradle of life.

From the start, these mountains had been sacred, a place of great spiritual power. As a small boy, Oro himself had climbed their heights in a vision quest. The spirits had smiled on him and granted him the powers of an *izze-nantan*, a medicine man. Then he and his people had pierced the mountains' very heart as if with a great arrow. They had dug into its rock, gutting its soul. Rather than accept death, they had helped greedy Spaniards find *pesh-litzogue*, the yellow iron.

Even after Oro's father had led an uprising that had wiped out their captors, the *Shis-Inday* had passed up a chance to make up for their sins. For days, Oro's father had directed efforts to dislodge a great jumble of rocks that capped the mountain of *pesh-litzogue*. Finally, a lone boulder had stood poised for the push that would start a landslide and seal the mine's entrance, a hundred feet below.

But too many braves had given up the old beliefs in favor of a new idea. In their months of captivity, they had learned the power of the yellow iron. In it they had seen the means to get weapons so they could drive the Spanish invaders from their land. The temptation had proved too great, and the warriors had murdered Oro's father right in front of the boy's eyes.

Still, the braves had never claimed *pesh-litzogue* for their own. The spirits had been too quick with terrible judgment.

In the face of growling spirits and the vengeful ghosts of Spaniards, Oro and the warriors had fled through mountains alive with devil animals. It had all been so terrifying that no Apache, not even Oro, had ever dared ride this trail again.

With the passing of many winters, only Oro had remained alive to remember these things. Yet he had kept the secret of *pesh-litzogue* to himself. Too many warriors had lost faith in the old teachings about the cradle of life. They wanted only to strip the mountains of the yellow iron and hasten the bloody flow.

Oro was gone now. But Child-of-the-Waters suddenly seemed to feel him strong at his side. The boy would need a medicine man's strength, and more, if the white youths ever led him to the mine. It would take a lot of courage to do what was right and seal it. After all, such a deed would forever disgrace him in the eyes of the warriors.

He found the gorge floor gently sloping and thick with greenery. There were pinyon pine, drooping juniper, mountain oak, and ash. To any desert dweller, it was an oasis, especially with the sound of trickling water coming from somewhere ahead. He could already feel the dampness in the air and smell the moist earth.

A monarch butterfly floated by as he neared a twisted alligator juniper. He ducked under the hanging limbs and saw something at his shoulder that gave him pause. There were fresh scratches on the tree's thick, scaly bark. He thought he recognized them as the claw marks of *shoz-dijiji*, the black bear. In the Sierra del Carmen, the animal was usually shy, fearing man above all else. Unless protecting its young, it was rarely a threat. But given what Oro had told Child-of-the-Waters about the Chisos, he wasn't so sure anymore.

Suddenly he wished for as many metal-tipped arrows as his hand could hold.

He went on, trying to curb his fear. Soon he parted a tangle of greenery and broke upon a small clearing thirty steps across. Ahead and to his left loomed a tepee-sized boulder, a massive rock dome covered with yellow-green lichen. A long, deep crack zigzagged down its face. Near the crest, the crevice was only a fracture, but it began to widen halfway to the ground.

The dark slit would have made a good lair for a small animal, thought Child-of-the-Waters. But the squeeze way was blocked at bottom by a rough column of rock standing as tall as he.

He took all of this in with a glance as he angled across the clearing with its clumps of sotol and basket grass. His course carried him within an arm's length of the boulder. As he came abreast of the deep crack, a sudden chill swept over him. He looked back over his shoulder. It was as if he could feel eyes upon him. But all he found was a wall of greenery along the curve of the clearing.

Suddenly brush began to rustle, freezing him in his tracks. There was no sun to face for its blessing, so he didn't hesitate as he whirled to the clearing's lower end. Not far inside the crowding thicket, dry leaves were crackling. Then a twig snapped sharply, and foliage began to stir. Limbs were moving! There was something in there—something big—and it was coming right at him!

He turned to flee and ran straight into a white boy coming around the boulder.

"Ah-yee!" cried Child-of-the-Waters.

"Yee-ah!" cried the *pindah-lickoyee*.

Suddenly neither boy could breathe. But they had plenty of spring in their legs. Both of them jumped like *ka-chu* the jackrabbit.

For a split second, Child-of-the-Waters looked wide-eyed at the white eyes, and the white eyes looked back. It was the closest the Apache boy had ever been to a *pindah-lickoyee*. He never wanted to be this close again.

Tensing, he started to bolt.

Suddenly a deep, angry whine and the snap of jaws brought him wheeling. If he had been scared before, he was petrified now. A monster of a bear, longer than a man, was breaking through the last shielding brush. This was no *shoz-dijiji*, no timid black bear rooting for grubs. The thick hump above its shoulders and the white tips in its brown, shaggy fur told a different story—a terrifying one.

It was a grizzly, a man-killer!

CHAPTER 12

Child-of-the-Waters had never before seen a grizzly, the most feared of all bears. But Alchesay had told him about its great strength and terrible ways. A full-grown grizzly was heavier than a war horse and almost as fast. It had long, sharp claws that could open a deer's belly with one swipe. A single blow from its powerful forelegs could crush a horse's skull. A warrior who found himself stalked might well escape its limited eyesight, but not its other senses. This one's sharp ears and unerring nose had led it straight to Child-of-the-Waters.

He knew that from so short a distance even a crippled grizzly could run him down in moments. And this one looked all too healthy, despite a deep scar across its snout.

The monster raised up on its hind legs and roared. But somehow Child-of-the-Waters curbed his fear as a warrior should. It gave him the presence of mind to whirl and seize the standing rock that blocked the boulder's deep crack. He tugged on the tall stone with all his might, knowing that the crevice behind was his only chance.

It wouldn't budge!

He grimaced and threw a shoulder into it, and the pillar continued to hold fast. He gave a primal cry and called upon the Great Spirit *Usen*, and still the column only rocked.

He heard the bear roar again, then another set of hands joined his on the pillar. Suddenly, the white eyes was fighting as hard as he to upend it. They were enemies, this *Shis-inday* and *pindah-lickoyee*. But they were working side-by-side to do what neither could do alone.

The standing rock teetered on edge. The grizzly charged. The column crashed down with a rumble and a burst of dust. The boys lunged for the crack as the bear sprang for the kill. The cleft was so narrow that the *pindah-lickoyee* could only wedge himself in sideways. Child-of-the-Waters was at his shoulder, squeezing through just ahead of a fierce swipe of claws.

The white eyes slammed into the back wall, and Child-of-the-Waters threw himself up against him. They were barely deeper than the length of a man's arm. The novice spun around to the shaft of light and came face-to-face with an enraged grizzly. He could see down its throat and count its dripping fangs. He could smell its musky breath and see the madness burning in its eyes.

It was a devil animal, just like the bobcat. But this one was a thousand times stronger.

The grizzly hurled itself against the crack, trying to force its way in. It drove a foreleg in up to the shoulder and pawed with its knife-like claws. Child-of-the-Waters tried to shrink back even more, but there was no place to go. He could only suck in his stomach until his navel seemed pinned to his spine. Still, the raking claws came so close that they shredded the water pouches dangling against his ribs.

The grizzly's inability to reach Child-of-the-Waters enraged the monster even more. It roared right in Child-of-the-Water's ears. It snapped at the rock with its powerful jaws. It tore at the crack with its free claws, sending shards of rock flying. Child-of-the-Waters feared that even this great boulder couldn't stand up to the might of a devil bear. Little by little, the grizzly was widening the cleft. Another few moments and it would reach him with those terrible claws.

Suddenly the grizzly twitched from the shoulder up and squalled loudly. Withdrawing its claws, it began shaking its head violently and pawing at its neck. Moments before, this merciless predator had seemed so immune to discomfort. Now it looked to be in the throes of pain.

With his narrow field of vision, Child-of-the-Waters could only see in glimpses. Whining and roaring, the bear tossed its shaggy head back and forth across the jag of daylight. A couple of times Child-of-the-Waters thought he could make out something dark and wet clinging to the grizzled fur. Then the bear twisted its head right before him and the Apache boy saw a feathered shaft in its neck.

The grizzly shuddered a second time, then a third. As it dropped, partially blocking the opening, Child-of-the-Waters saw two more arrows side-by-side under its shoulder.

Suddenly the bear was still. Not even a breath of wind stirred its white-tipped fur. Child-of-the-Waters prayed it was dead.

Still, the Apache boy was afraid to move. He was afraid to breathe even. The grizzly devil might come to life again and finish what it had started.

"Child-of-the-Waters! Is that you in the rock, Child-of-the-Waters?"

He knew the voice well.

"I'm here, Loco!" the novice called out.

"Why are you still hiding like a lizard?"

Child-of-the-Waters no longer had to prove his courage to himself. But he did to Loco. "I wanted to stand and fight the great bear *dijiji*! But I didn't have a warrior's sharp arrows!"

A silhouette appeared in the shaft of light. "My arrows are sharp and full of medicine too!" bragged the warrior. "No one but Loco could have bent the bow that drove them into the great bear's heart! *Yah-tats-an*! Look, it's dead now! Come out and see what Loco does to his enemies!"

With a muffled war whoop, the warrior drew his knife and fell to work slashing the bear's carcass.

Child-of-the-Waters started to edge out, then hesitated. At his shoulder was a *pindah-lickoyee*—and not just any *pindah-lickoyee*. This was the boy who had spoken with Oro in the language without words. He had tended the *izze-nantan* in his dying minutes. For two and a half days now, the warriors had tracked him. This white eyes and his companions were the Apaches' only hope of ever finding *pesh-litzogue*.

Maybe the three young whites knew where the yellow iron was, and maybe they didn't. But Loco believed that torturing them was the best way to find out.

Only Alchesay had kept the cruel warrior from doing so up till now. On into the mountains, Alchesay's decision to track had seemed justified. The white youths had ridden a trail that had promised to lead to *pesh-litzogue*. Now all of that was in question.

Child-of-the-Waters knew what would happen if Loco discovered the white boy. With Alchesay's plans suddenly dashed, Loco would set to work tormenting the youth. Even now the warrior seemed to be practicing as he slashed at the grizzly's paws with his knife, removing the claws.

Child-of-the-Waters knew that *Usen* had never commanded his people to love their enemies. Apaches were to fight and even torture a foe for his wrongs. But this white eyes was no enemy. He had befriended Oro in his last moments. He had dragged him into the shade and bathed his forehead. He had watched over the kindly old *izze-nantan* to his final breath and then buried him the white man's way.

Not only that, but this white eyes and Child-of-the-Waters were brothers now, in a sense. Together they had worked to escape the great devil bear. They had struggled side-by-side against a common foe that would have killed them both. He owed this *pindah-lickoyee* his very life, and this *pindah-lickoyee* owed Child-of-the-Waters his. Even now, they stood shoulder-to-shoulder, brothers in an event that had done more than shape their future. It had given them one.

No, this white eyes was no enemy. If Child-of-the-Waters extended the hand of friendship further, maybe his white brother would still lead them to *pesh-litzogue*. Maybe Child-of-the-Waters himself could stop the bloody flow.

He looked around and searched the shadows for the boy's eyes. The Apache youth could see so little, and yet suddenly he could see so much.

He turned and worked his way toward daylight. Moments later he crawled out on the warm, sticky hide of the grizzly. On its very shoulder he stood, careful to keep his back against the crack. He waited there, hiding his white brother, while Loco finished his work. Soon, Child-of-the-Waters was following after the warrior as they started for camp. But the boy didn't leave the clearing without looking back at the dark cleft. In the language without words, he flashed a quick sign and then was away into the brush.

· •) ≋ (• ·

If fright could have been traded for dollars, Fish wouldn't have needed to search for lost gold anymore.

He waited in the crack long after the Apache boy and warrior were gone. When he finally found the courage to crawl out across the dead grizzly, it was far into dusk. He hurried down-canyon, sacrificing stealth for haste. There were too many dangers in this gorge in daylight. He didn't want to face more in the dark.

He dwelled on things as he pushed through the timber. The Apache boy had spared him. The youth had held his tongue and shielded him from the warrior's scalp knife. Fish wondered if he understood why.

Go in peace to the yellow iron!

The young Indian's sign had been clear. Somehow he knew what they were hunting for! But Fish was even more amazed by the contact that two human beings had made in a world of hatred and violence. They had joined in a fight against overwhelming odds. Alone, each of them would have met a horrible end. When the bear had fallen and the Apache had crawled into the open, he had kept quiet about him out of friendship.

It all reminded Fish so much of a Comanche boy he had once known. That bond had spared the lives of many Indians and white people. He wondered if this one would lead anywhere.

When Fish burst upon camp at dark, Punk was sprawled lazily at a crackling fire. He was twirling a straw in his teeth and wiggling his bare toes at the flames. Across from him, Gid was busy with a couple of tins down in the coals.

"Get that fire out!" Fish cried in a hushed voice.

"Say what?" asked Punk, looking around.

"The fire! You can see it for miles!"

"So?" quizzed the wrangler. "You can hear ol' Gid's stomach a-growlin' durn near that far too. Sounds like a regular tomcat a-purrin'. Makes me plum' hungry just listenin' to it. Say, ain't that food smellin' tasty! Can't wait to wrap my poor ol' tongue around it!"

"Doggone it, quit your yappin'!" exclaimed Fish. "We got trouble!"

"What's ailin' you so?" asked Gid.

Fish rushed over and began kicking dirt in the fire, forcing Punk to reel in his toes.

"Hey!" complained the wrangler. "What in Sam Hill you doin' to ol' Punk's supper?"

"We gotta get outa here! There's Indians—Apaches! They know we're after that ol' mine!"

Now Punk wasn't so casual about things anymore. He sprang to his feet, forgetting he had no boots on. "Yeow!" he exclaimed, dancing around tender-footed. "Indians? Where'd you see Indians?"

Fish continued spraying the fire with dirt. "Up yonder in that gorge!"

"I'll be a monkey-faced owl! Wonder if them's the same ones from this mornin'!"

"What ones from this mornin'?" asked Gid.

"Stop talkin' and start saddlin'!" urged Fish. "We gotta ride! Pa told me Apaches don't like to fight at night! Come mornin', they liable to be all over us!"

CHAPTER 13

They struck out through the night, young cowboys riding a haunted trail up Juniper Canyon.

Back at that clearing, Fish had watched the two Indians start away toward the canyon's mouth. So that had driven the three boys deeper in the Chisos. Maybe, just maybe, they would find a pass up and over these spooky crags.

As they rode, talking in hushed tones, Fish told of the Apache boy and the grizzly.

"How is it you're always gettin' chummy with some wild Indian?" asked Gid. "First Hunting Bear, and now this. How come they don't scalp you like they near done me that time?"

"Maybe they don't like that rat's nest he calls his hair," suggested Punk. "Say, if it takes a grizzly breathin' down your neck to get cozy with some redskin, you fellers can just leave ol' Punk out anyhow."

The terrain was so broken and the night so black that the miles only crawled by. In the dark of the morning, they struck a sharp slope at canyon's head. Way up against the stars, Fish could see the skyline of a natural saddle between a cathedral of rock and a timbered mountain.

For the first time since he had been in this canyon, Fish knew where he was. Oro had described this place, and from the old mission Fish had seen it for himself. From the saddle, it would be an easy climb up the timbered mountain on the right. Over its crest would be a gorge and then a greater mountain. That far peak promised to bear a crown of rock—the very point that had caught the first rays of Easter.

A legend was waiting up there, and suddenly it seemed so real, so easy to have. Even the Apache boy had told him to go ahead. Gold! It could really be his, if he just had the courage!

And the greed.

Fish was elated, but he was troubled too. There were a lot of people in the world but just one who could find those lost diggings. But Oro hadn't shared that secret with him so he could scavenge it like a grave robber. Oro had sent him on a mission. He was to journey to that cursed place and heal the mountains' wound.

Whatever that meant exactly, it was important enough for Oro to have spent his dying breaths begging him to do it. That's why Fish was so troubled. With knowledge had come responsibility, a lot of it. So what was a boy to do?

He thought about his father, as he always did in trying times. His pa had been a good man, a righteous one. He had taught Fish integrity and honor and the importance of being true to himself and to others. Fish could almost hear his strong voice even now, as if he rode at his very side.

"A man ain't to steal or go off chasin' rainbows. He's to take only what he's got comin'. If he ain't done a honest day's work for somethin', it ain't his. It's the way the Good Lord intended it."

So where did all this leave Papa Guy, who faced such money woes right now?

Fish wasn't sure. But Papa Guy was a man of character, just like Fish's pa had been. Would he even want any gold that Fish got by betraying somebody's trust? Would he even accept something he hadn't broken a sweat for?

While Fish pondered things, the horses were climbing. From here it must have been five hundred feet up to that saddle, and the ponies were already struggling. The rocky slope was just too steep, and there were a lot of boulders and lechuguilla spears to work past. For a while, Fish tried to stay in the saddle. Then the angle grew so severe that the boys dismounted and led their animals up a frightful landslide channel.

It was a desperate climb, but they were desperate boys.

Just as the sun came up, they pushed tiredly up through rimrock and gained the saddle. It was a narrow ridge, and on the far side was a right-to-left canyon with towering cliffs behind. Not far down its forested bottom, a deep notch split those rocky heights. On through it to the north, the land sloped gently toward a broken desert and distant crags.

"You seein' what I'm seein'?" Gid asked excitedly as they held their horses.

Fish was seeing plenty. This was exactly the pass through these mountains the boys had hoped for.

"We're home free, fellers!" bellowed Punk. "Ain't a dozen miles across there to headquarters!"

"You reckon Ma's worried sick about us?" asked Fish.

"I just hope she ain't too riled, long as we been gone," replied Gid. "You and your big ideas!"

"If I was you fellers," spoke up Punk, "I'd brace myself for a good hug and then a powerful lickin'. Either way, it's bound to be better than what them Indians had in mind."

"Reckon they's a-followin' us, Punk?" Fish asked.

"Even if they is, I reckon we got half a day's jump on 'em, hard as it was gettin' up here. I reckon we can take our own sweet time from here on. Say, wouldn't a few minutes of shut-eye be good right now!"

But Fish's attention was suddenly fixed on the timbered mountain that formed the rear of the saddle. Abruptly he was struck with all kinds of temptation. That gold mine was up there somewhere, just waiting. Almost a century had passed since anybody had laid eyes on it. It was the greatest mystery of the whole Big Bend, and it was suddenly Fish's to solve.

He was dying for a peek at that gold. If he didn't take any, what harm would there be in just looking? With the Apaches so far behind, the three of them would have plenty of time. They could take a quick look, leave things as they were, and then beat it for home.

Or so he told himself.

"So what do y'all think about things?" he mused, holding his stare at that mountain.

"Well, I'm a-thinkin' how good a plate of beans would be right now," said Punk. "Ummm! And some sourdough biscuits! You reckon ol' Grunt will have anything cooked up when we come ridin' in?"

"That ain't what I'm talkin' about. Y'all still wanna find that lost mine?"

"Well," said Punk, as skeptical as ever, "I do still kinda have a hankerin' for that skunk sandwich. Figure I can sit right there on them piles of gold and eat it."

"How come you askin' all of a sudden?" quizzed Gid. "What you lookin' at up there?"

"The way to Oro's gold."

For the first time in a lot of long, hard miles, Punk roared with laughter. "I swear, I'm gonna hate it when this trip ends!

Y'all are more fun than a barrel of rats in a house full of women folk!"

"Fish?" pressed Gid. "You really think it's up that way? How far?"

"An hour or two. We're that close, Gid! What do you think?"

"A couple of hours? You sure?"

"Not any more than that! Come on! What do you say?"

The sudden fire in Gid's eyes said it all. "Let's stake these horses out of sight! I can't wait to see it! A gold mine! A real gold mine! Wait'll I tell Papa!"

Fish could hardly contain his excitement as he turned to the wrangler. "Punk?"

The older youth flashed one of those grins that could bring a raccoon out of a tree. "Lead the way, Fish ol' boy! You think ol' Punk would pass up a skunk sandwich?"

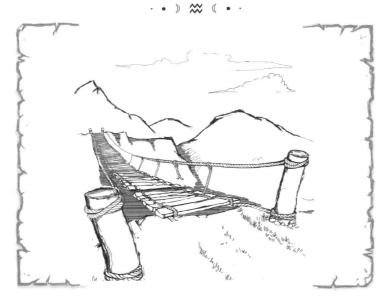

CHAPTER 14

"I ain't a-crossin' no hundred-year-old bridge! If I was to fall down there, all the gold in California couldn't put me back together again!"

Gid had a point. They had just broken out of a summit forest of pinyon pines and crossed a brief lip of solid rock. Now they stood at a swinging foot bridge that spanned a narrow gorge with sheer cliffs. Five hundred feet straight down, Fish could see the tops of ponderosa pines and Arizona cypresses. It was a long drop, all right, all the way to a quick grave. But Fish hadn't struggled up another exhausting slope for grins. That eighty-foot bridge joined with a mountain of lost treasure.

Gold! It was right across there! His excitement grew to a fever pitch as he lifted his gaze up that mighty rise. It must have reached another thousand feet into the sky. Even from a peak as high as this, Fish felt dwarfed by it. He studied every rock outcrop and patch of green forest, every jagged spire and soaring cliff. They were all so awe-inspiring. Yet one feature captured his imagination as nothing else did—the summit.

It was a bulging cap of boulders, a crazy-quilt jumble of stone that ruled over a whole mountain.

For a moment Fish was back at those mud walls. He was standing in the dawn, watching the rising sun burn against a single bump on the faraway Chisos. In a sneeze, it had all been over. For a lot of tough miles, there had been nothing but a fading memory of it and a distant dream. Now, just a few yards of wobbly bridge stood between him and the greatest secret of the ages.

He inspected the structure. Only a few feet wide, it was swung by ropes thicker than a man's arm. Split juniper limbs, laid crossway, formed the floor. On each side were widely spaced posts that joined the deck with upper support ropes running shoulder-high.

All the ropes looked plenty frayed, and the decking was just as weathered. Some timbers had rotted out completely, giving the bridge the look of a grinning cowboy with missing teeth. But the most ominous thing about it was the way it creaked as it swung in the wind.

"I ain't goin' across that thing!" Gid said again.

"Does appear a mite rickety," offered Punk, looking it over. "I've chomped down on some of ol' Grunt's biscuits that was stouter than them timbers look."

"It ain't so bad," said Fish, doing some wishful thinking. "Papa Guy says things don't rot much in this dry climate. Besides, the Spaniards built this to last. It had to hold up burros loaded to the gills with ore. Anyhow, it just goes to prove there really is a mine up there. Who else would go and put a bridge here?"

He went closer and gave a tug on each upper rope. "Feels sturdy enough. Wonder how that floorin' is."

The first plank hovered over solid rock, so there was little risk. He tested it with his foot and his boot drove right through it.

"Whoa, boy!" exclaimed Punk, throwing out a rescuing hand. "We'll be a-scrapin' you up off that canyon floor!"

Fish backed away, shaken. But he was suddenly in the grip of a fever stronger than fear. He had to get across!

"Maybe it's just that one board, y'all," he said, edging to the side. He stooped for a look at the bridge's underbelly. "See how the dirt blowed in under it and rotted it out? Them other timbers don't look so bad."

But common sense would have told him that they didn't look so great either. He could see the underside all the way across. The bridge had quite a sag before it caught the far rim right over a dark keyhole in the whitewashed cliff. The small cave was only a few feet below several missing slats that would make those final steps plenty tricky.

He was still studying and dreaming. But he heard a couple of voices trying to talk some sense into him.

"Let's head for home," urged Gid.

"I expect we oughta, Fish ol' boy," joined in Punk. "My ol' tummy's gettin' plenty lank. You know, I—"

"Yeow!"

Punk and Gid hollered together. Fish spun. Not thirty feet behind them, a mountain lion with evil, green eyes crouched at forest's edge. The cat was huge, six and one-half feet of tawny muscle and thick tail. Everything about it—its hard stare, the angry look of its tight-set jaws, the twitch of that black-tipped tail—said it was about to attack. Fish expected nothing less. There were too many vengeful spirits burning in its eyes.

He didn't like his chances. Papa Guy had told him that a lion was faster then a deer for a short distance. Its powerful legs could carry it twenty feet in a bound. A boy could never outrun one, and if he tried, the outcome was certain. A panther's method was to pounce on its prey from behind and seize it with those wicked claws. As soon as the cat sunk its teeth in a victim's neck, it was all over.

Suddenly the panther was creeping closer. It was holding its deadly stare as its great paws padded on the rock.

"What are we gonna do!" exclaimed Gid, who looked ready to bolt.

"Stay still!" urged Fish.

"Still, my eye!" the wrangler exclaimed. "Look who's closest to him!"

Sure enough, they were bunched single file now: Punk in front, Gid in the middle, and Fish in back.

"You gotta do somethin', Punk!" urged Fish. "Talk to him! Calm him down!"

The wrangler sure wasn't laughing now. "What do you want ol' Punk to say to him? Here, kitty, kitty?"

As if on cue, the mountain lion inched closer. It was crowding them right off the cliff. Fish knew there was only one thing to do.

"Start backin'!" he hollered.

"What do you mean, start backin'!" exclaimed Gid. "There's a cliff back there!"

"If ol' Fish says go to backin', then go to backin'!" pleaded Punk, who was doing his best to retreat right through Gid. "I can already smell that kitty's breath, and he sure ain't brushed his teeth lately!"

They moved like a giant, six-legged bug, their boots doing a fast shuffle together across the rock. Suddenly the bridge was right at Fish's back.

"Y'all gotta watch your step!" he warned as he mounted the timbers.

Only now did Gid realize what Fish had in mind. Hemmed in behind the wrangler, Gid suddenly was pushing against Punk as hard as Punk was pushing against him.

"I told you I ain't goin' on this thing!" Gid cried.

Meanwhile, Punk's close-up view of the cat was only getting better.

"He ain't a-goin' on this thing, he said!" repeated the wrangler. "Well, if you'll just let ol' Punk by then, you and me both will be happy!"

Suddenly all three were on the bridge. They were gripping its upper ropes, feeling its sway, listening to it complain. Down between the cracks, Fish could see a lot of open air. There was nothing keeping them from a swan dive but a few groaning ropes and pitching timbers.

But things were only getting worse. There was a devil lifting a paw to join them on the bridge.

"Run along now, would you, Mister Kitty?" pleaded Punk as the three of them backed along. "Ain't you got some tom-cattin' around to do?"

But the panther had no intention of going away. It pounced on the timbers, and the added weight made the bridge sag and creak even more. The support posts on the rim suddenly had a mighty worrisome lean.

Baring its fangs, the great cat squalled fiercely. Fish had never seen so many sharp teeth, not even in the grizzly's mouth. The boys squalled back and quickened their retreat.

"There's missin' boards!" warned Fish.

Somehow the three avoided those awful gaps and reached mid-bridge. Here where the slack in the ropes was greatest, the side-to-side sway was at its extreme. The wind made it bad enough. But with every move they made, the bridge tossed all the more.

"I never did like swings!" exclaimed Gid. "They always made me throw up!"

"Well, I wish you'd turn your head before you do!" hollered the wrangler. "That's ol' Punk's shoulder you're droolin' on!"

The only good thing about the sway was that the mountain lion didn't seem to like it any better than they did. The cat had all but stopped now.

Suddenly it pricked its ears and looked back at the rim. Something had seized its attention. A moment later it was whirling and bounding away, rocking the bridge more than ever.

"Somethin's scared him!" exclaimed Fish, clinging to the side ropes for all he was worth.

"I ain't complainin'!" cried Punk. "Let him run to Jericho!"

The panther cleared the last dozen feet of bridge in a single leap and bolted into thick timber. Fish could still hear it rustling the brush when he caught a sudden glint of sunlight. It came from pinyon pines that hugged the rim a couple of hundred yards to his right. "You see that?" he asked in a hushed cry.

"Sun's a-hittin' somethin'!" whispered Gid.

"Not much that mad kitty would run from!" offered Punk.

"It's Indians!" exclaimed Fish. "It's gotta be Indians! The sun's flashin' off a spear point or somethin'! Ain't no critters gonna be carryin' anything shiny!"

"We're sittin' ducks out here!" cried Gid.

"More like sittin' turkeys!" corrected Punk. "But we sure gotta do somethin', fellers! Mighty quick!"

· •) ≋ (• ·

Child-of-the-Waters had never been so troubled.

Throughout the night they had trailed the white boys at a distance up the canyon. As day had broken at its head, the warriors had taken their ponies behind an outcrop. In secret, they had watched the youths on the saddle above strike out on foot. Then the braves had pushed their horses hard up a game trail and themselves even harder up the forested slope. Now Child-of-the-Waters and eight *Shis-Inday* warriors were padding through pinyon pines on a summit ridge.

Soon, perhaps, they would overtake the white eyes at *pesh-litzogue*. They would forget about not angering Oro's ghost. They would kill Child-of-the-Waters' white brother, seize the yellow iron for themselves alone, and bring terrible judgment on the world.

Child-of-the-Waters himself had encouraged his white brother to lead them here. But now the Apache boy just didn't know what to do.

Suddenly they broke out of the timber to face a creaking footbridge swaying furiously. How strange, thought the youth, that it pitched so much in a wind so gentle.

Then it struck him. It hadn't been the wind that had set that bridge in motion. It had been human legs—those of the three white eyes!

They were somewhere right across that gorge! They were headed for the yellow iron, and eight bloodthirsty warriors were on their tail!

Quickly Loco tested the bridge and started across. The warrior second in line waited for him to gain the far rim and then followed. One at a time, five more Apaches crossed the gorge, until only Alchesay and Child-of-the-Waters remained.

The boy knew what Alchesay was going to say even as the war chief turned.

"You'll stay here, Child-of-the-Waters."

The boy wanted to protest, but he was not permitted. As a Chisos Apache, he understood that a novice was to be kept out of harm's way. But he had to go! Events across that gorge would decide everything! His white brother would die, and the warriors would drain the cradle of life of its lifeblood! It would mean the end of all things! The mountains, the sky, the earth—*everything*! He had to get across and stop the bloody flow before it was too late!

Alchesay crossed, and Child-of-the-Waters was suddenly alone with his thoughts. How could he just stand here and let all that he knew would happen, happen? Didn't he owe more than that to his people, to Oro, to his white brother?

Within minutes everything was decided for him. He turned at the snapping of twigs and saw a mountain lion not twenty feet away. Its eyes were on fire with the same madness he had seen in the devil bear.

The great cat squalled, and Child-of-the-Waters backed onto the bridge. He reached for a novice's arrow and nocked it to his bow. The panting lion slunk closer, and the boy drew the sinew string back. He had never bent a bow so far. Yet when he let the arrow fly, its blunt point bounced harmlessly off the lion's thick hide.

But it did have an effect. It enraged the cat, driving it to the attack. It leaped on the bridge after him, setting the structure rocking wildly. Child-of-the-Waters could barely hold on. But one good thing came out of the careen. The mountain lion stopped its charge and dug its claws in the timbers.

But not for long. Even as the bridge kept up its alarming sway, the panther came at him with fierce swipes of those claws.

Child-of-the-Waters slid back along the ropes faster than safety allowed. There were terrible holes underfoot, a pawing mountain lion at his chest, and vengeful spirits all about. Never had an Apache boy faced such terrors. But he had to keep from panicking. Fear could drive him to a misstep and send him plummeting. If that happened, a lot more than his own little world would come to an end.

After the longest minute of his life, Child-of-the-Waters found himself right over the keyhole cave in the far cliff. Suddenly the screaming cat was crowding him more than ever. Its claws lashed out and shredded his leather shirt. The boy lunged back, groping with his foot for a timber that wasn't there. The next thing he knew, his leg was plunging through a gaping hole.

He cried out as his hips followed. He slapped his arms left and right, catching the bottom ropes on each side. But he was in trouble, big trouble! One leg was hooked across a timber, but the rest of him just dangled! Knife-like claws were raking his moccasin, and he was about to fall all the way to the gorge floor!

All at once something seized his swinging leg. A voice called out with words he didn't understand. Several hands gripped his torso from below, buoying him up. Just as the cougar began sinking fangs in his moccasin, he lost his hold and slipped on through with a cry.

The drag of his leg across the timber threw the bridge into a vicious roll. Nothing could have ridden it out. Just as hands pulled Child-of-the-Waters into the cave, the squalling devil cat pitched headlong past him.

Child-of-the-Waters had escaped the terrible fall. But what manner of awful spirits gripped him now?

CHAPTER 15

"**I** don't know what we're doin' savin' a wild Indian!" Gid exclaimed in a hushed voice. "They's out to scalp us!"

The boys had just dragged the Apache youth with the ripped shirt and mangled moccasin inside the cave. Gid and Punk were eyeing him cautiously as he came to his feet.

"Look out! He's gonna try somethin'!" Gid went on.

"This one ain't!" said Fish. "If he was gonna scalp me, he could've did it yesterday! We fought that grizzly off together! Him and me's friends, just like me and Hunting Bear!"

"Yeah? Well, I bet this one's got some mean kinfolk that'll be huntin' him!"

"Sure as shootin'," agreed Punk. "Say, next time you fellers get a hankerin' to play hide-and-seek with a bunch of Indians, y'all can just leave ol' Punk behind."

The narrow cave with its jagged rock and musty smell had been a godsend to the boys. It was high enough to stand in and dark enough to hide them from the bridge. But just before the panther had shown up again, Fish had made out faint twilight far in its depths. Now he faced the keyhole of daylight and the Apache boy who stood in silhouette.

Fish pointed to himself and gestured. "I'm Fish, son of a cowboy."

The Apache boy cast wary eyes at Gid and Punk before responding in the language without words.

"Child-of-the-Waters. I know you, Fish-Son-of-a-Cowboy."

"We whipped that ol' bear together."

"The devil cat too. We're brothers in battle. The two of us."

"What's he a-sayin'?" quizzed Gid. "Me and Punk don't know that sign lingo."

Fish waved his cousin off and addressed the Apache boy again. "What's your people up to, anyhow? They out to scalp us?"

"They think the *izze-nantan* told you how to get to the yellow iron. They'll wait till you lead them there. Then they'll draw their knives."

Fish swallowed hard and looked at Gid and Punk.

"Come on!" pleaded Gid. "Tell us what he's sayin'!"

"From the look on that puss of his, it ain't good, I'll tell you that," observed Punk. "I've seen happier looks when ol' Grunt was after him with a fryin' pan."

"Oro," the Apache boy said aloud. Then he resumed his gestures. "Did he really tell you the secret he wouldn't tell anybody else?"

"Oro?" repeated Gid. "What's all this got to do with that ol' Indian?"

When Fish didn't answer Child-of-the-Waters immediately, the Apache continued. "We watched you with the *izze-nantan*. You talked to him in the language without words, but we were a long way off. We saw him point to the Chisos and die. Did he really tell you how to find *pesh-litzogue?*"

Fish only looked at him. But the answer must have been written all over the young cowboy's face.

"What will you do when you get there?" asked Child-of-the-Waters.

"I . . . I ain't sure," Fish answered truthfully.

"The warriors think *pesh-litzogue* will buy them rifles and make our people strong again. But the yellow iron is cursed. Did Oro tell you?"

Suddenly a terrible chill worked its way down Fish's backbone. "He said I needed to heal up these mountains somehow, that their spirits was angry. But he died before he could tell me how."

"I can still hear Oro's whispers. I know how!"

Stunned, Fish could suddenly do nothing but stare. He was already involved in a mystery bigger than these mountains. Now he felt himself being drawn into something bigger than his whole imagination.

"Yeow! This place is crawlin' with scorpions!" Gid suddenly cried. "Look out—they's all over your arm!"

Fish whirled. Gid was right. Half a dozen scorpions were on his tattered sleeve. He reeled back, brushing at them with a frantic hand.

"They's a-comin' outa the walls like ants to a picnic!" exclaimed Punk, dancing a sudden jig. "We gotta get outa here!"

But Gid had already poked his head out into the light and was peering up at the foot bridge. "Gettin' down from there's one thing! Gettin' back up's somethin' else! I—I ain't sure we can do it!"

While the three white eyes were panicking, Child-of-the-Waters was studying. He knew how difficult it would be to regain that bridge in a hurry. But as his eyes had adjusted to the gloom, he had noticed the eerie twilight far back in the rock. He nudged Fish and pointed. Then he rushed away into the cave's depths.

"He's leadin' us outa here!" Fish cried. "Come on, let's go!"

They did a lot of feeling in the dark and some fancy squirming up through some tight passages. But finally they zigzagged back to a crawlway that angled up sharply toward daylight. Child-of-the-Waters slithered out first, but Fish was right behind. The young cowboy was brushing scorpions off even as he popped out into open air.

The daylight was so blinding and the rocky ground so steep that he stayed on hands and knees to get his bearings. He was in a chiseled canyon that climbed the face of the treasure mountain. Knobby cliffs squeezed in from both sides, dwarfing the scrub brush around him. Ahead, the narrow canyon rose so quickly that its slope soon bent out of sight.

Suddenly Fish's skin began crawling in a way that it hadn't since he had read an old Indian's dying gestures.

He wasn't welcome here, something told him. Nobody was.

Against the sky up-canyon, towers of rock looked down on him like angry spirits waiting to punish. The pinnacles were catching plenty of howling wind—or was it the wailing of ghosts he heard? Gold or no gold, that was one place he didn't intend to go. Even where he knelt, the very earth seemed to shake and moan.

"Them stingin' lizards is still all over me!"

In one way, Gid's muffled cry from down in the hole was a relief. The ground was rumbling all right. But it was the sound of two frantic boys wriggling up that squeeze way.

"Papa says they burn just like a hot iron!" Gid went on.

"I just hope they ain't the Arizony kind!" added Punk. "They say them can kill a feller dead!"

Just as Fish started to rise, the Apache boy's sudden hand on his shoulder made him pause. Fish looked around. Child-of-the-Waters had a finger across his lips. There was terrible concern in his eyes as he nodded down the mountain.

Fish turned and looked downwind. Where the canyon bluffs opened up forty yards away, a tall juniper stump stood on a dome of rock.

Fish shuddered.

Against the dead tree reared a great spotted cat. It was clawing the scaly bark and rubbing its face into it. The panther at the bridge had been monster enough, but this beast was Satan himself. Those claw marks must have been seven feet up!

Papa Guy had told Fish that jaguars—"tigers" to the Mexicans—sometimes came up from Mexico. But this was the first that Fish had ever seen. He had never looked upon an animal so stunning. The jaguar's coat was a deep gold with rose-like patterns of black. Its velvety fur rippled with every flex of its powerful muscles. It looked so proud and kingly.

But it was an evil beauty. This cat was a natural-born killer, cunning and always on the hunt. Every time Papa Guy had told him about tigers, Fish had tossed and turned half the night. Now he remembered all about those mighty jaws that could bring down a full-grown buffalo or crush a man's skull. But this jaguar wasn't just a picture in his mind. It was a deadly threat just a stone's throw away!

Fish spun to give warning to Punk and Gid. But the boys were already hollering in alarm as they spilled out of the hole.

"Brush 'em off ol' Punk! Brush 'em off!"

"They's all over me! Get em off, y'all! Get 'em off!"

"Shhh!"

Fish's whisper came too late. As the squinting boys paled in alarm, he turned to face the jaguar. The cat looked straight at him as it dropped into a crouch and froze. Suddenly it seemed more than predator. Behind those piercing, yellow-green eyes lurked every mad spirit on this whole mountain.

"He sees us!" he cried under his breath.

"Jeepers! Is that a tiger?" asked Gid.

"Whatever it is, ol' Punk don't wanna have nothin' to do with it!"

The moment Punk began clambering away up the steep canyon, the jaguar's tail began to twitch. Suddenly its every muscle was like a tightly coiled spring. It spread its jaws, and a deep growl rumbled up from its throat.

"Look out! He's gonna come on up!" exclaimed Fish.

He spun, not knowing what to do. The cave was just feet away, but so were all those scorpions. Maybe they weren't the Arizona kind at all. But he figured enough stings from the Texas variety could kill a person just as dead.

Suddenly Child-of-the-Waters was tugging on his arm and pointing up the canyon. Gid was already bolting up it on all fours. Before Fish had drawn another breath, he was scrambling after his cousin with the Indian boy at his side.

He looked back and didn't like what he saw. The cat was eyeing their every move and slinking closer. Jumping Jehoshaphat! A tiger was stalking them!

The footing was loose, forcing Fish to run three steps to make two. They hurtled up past twisted junipers and through a water-hewn chute of rock. They pushed hard up a gravelly slide and over several rock shelves. When Fish and Child-of-the-Waters finally looked back, the canyon's lower reaches were hidden by the curve of the slope.

"I don't see him no more!" exclaimed Gid as he paused in front of Fish.

"Maybe he—"

Fish's words died in a throaty growl that echoed between the bluffs.

He turned to Gid. "Go! Go!" he hollered, giving his cousin a quick boost up.

Now Fish barreled up the incline more recklessly than ever. That growl could have come from anywhere! Even right below those junipers, or under that rock shelf! Any moment that cat could run him down!

He had been so caught up in escaping that he hadn't realized he was going right up to a place he didn't have any desire to go. But now the wail of that ghostly wind was growing louder. The rock spirits were getting closer, just like the secret to a legend that was all but forgotten now. His life was on the line!

For minutes that seemed hours, they frantically stumbled up a haunted mountain. By the time they reached a big landslide channel, they were dog-tired and breathless. They sprawled exhausted in the rocks after checking for signs of pursuit. Before Fish could breathe a sigh of relief, Child-of-the-Waters seized his arm.

The Apache pointed skyward. "The spirits are all around us!" he said in the language without words.

Sure enough, all those jutting stone figures loomed right over the boys. In shape, the hundred-foot pinnacles were man-like. But in detail they were nothing less than hideous. They seemed to have the faces of devils as they stared down, guarding a century-old secret.

They almost seemed alive. Maybe it was because their very height made them appear to move against the sky. Maybe it was because they wailed as the wind whipped between their summits. Either way, it made Fish wish he hadn't ever seen that old Indian.

"What in tarnation is that? The wind a-howlin'?" asked Gid.

"That's ol' Punk a-cryin'!" whimpered the wrangler. "He could be lappin' up cobbler and burpin' somewheres right now! But no, he's gotta traipse off with you yay-hoos! He's gotta crawl up a mountain full of wild Indians and serve hisself up for breakfast to a hair ball bigger than Texas!"

Fish turned his gaze on up the slope. He hadn't realized before just how high they had climbed. They were out of the canyon now and clinging to the mountain's upper reaches. The uppermost cliffs hung in the sky not three hundred eagle-flight feet above him. Another hundred feet higher and an eagle could perch right on that crazy quilt of boulders at the peak's summit.

All of a sudden everything that Oro had told him raced through his mind.

They were almost there.

The legend, the secret, the lost gold of the Chisos—they were almost there.

But suddenly, so was a man-eating jaguar.

CHAPTER 16

· •) ≋ (• ·

Gid was up with a cry. He was scrambling up the slope, and so was Punk. There was a hand yanking on Fish's arm, bringing him out of his thoughts.

"Run like *ittindi* the lightning!"

Fish didn't understand Child-of-the-Waters' words. But the low growl that came from behind was all too clear. Fish looked around even as he bolted. The jaguar was just a few hammering heartbeats behind and closing fast. It bounded right up that sharp rise with more grace than a deer. But to a boy running for his life, the cat's fluid motion was the most horrid thing he had ever seen.

Again and again Fish dug his boots into the sloughing gravel and scratched at it with his fingernails. He moaned and grunted and prayed, but he was fighting a losing battle. Every time he glanced back, he found the great cat gaining.

He scrambled higher and higher as he waited for those sharp claws to seize him. For yard after terrible yard, he fought to delay those crushing jaws. His pa would have expected nothing less of him.

But as a terrifying minute passed, something odd happened—nothing. He looked back. The jaguar was as close as ever and its piercing eyes were just as purposeful. But now it was slinking after him in almost casual fashion.

Tigers just don't do this way! he thought. Papa Guy says they sneak up and pounce in a hurry!

But Fish knew that this was more than a tiger. It was a swarm of avenging spirits toying with him, like a house cat with a mouse. Any time they wanted, they could run him down and take him in those jaws. But the teasing fiends chose to prolong the chase. They were delighting too much in his feeble attempts to get away.

Fish had never felt so sorry for a mouse.

Just then Punk and Gid cut sharply up and away toward the sun. Within moments Fish and Child-of-the-Waters joined them on a faint trail. It was steep and rocky and badly eroded. But for the first time in ages, Fish was up off his all fours.

He didn't figure it would make much difference.

The trail twisted around to the mountain's south face and carried the stampeding boys onto a shoulder. The thirty-foot summit cliffs were still well above. But on Fish's right was an abrupt fist of rock that jutted twenty feet or more. This one too had features that were both human-like and grotesque. Fish reckoned it for another rock spirit looking for revenge.

It was doing its part. It was resisting Punk's and Gid's frenzied efforts to scale it.

"They ain't no holds!" hollered the wrangler.

A quick look back told Fish that the tiger was through playing. It was closing with every stride!

"The cliffs!" he hollered. "It's all the chance we got!"

Far past exhaustion, the four struck out on hands and feet right up the loose slope. They had left the trail behind, but not the jaguar. The great cat was springing up agilely behind them. It was already so close that Fish's churning boots were spraying it with gravel as he brought up the rear.

Faster! He had to go faster! Those cliffs were up there and maybe hand holds that could save them!

But now Fish couldn't even see the bluffs. The slope overhead had too much of a bulge. Even the summit boulders were nearly hidden, but their eerie moan was as clear as the jaguar's growl. His common sense told him that it was just the wind whipping through those mighty rocks. But his heart knew better. It told him that it was the wail of angry spirits and lost souls.

Within yards, the incline grew so steep that Fish's flight became a real climb. Suddenly he could almost feel the jaguar breathing down his neck. Sheer panic gave him one last burst of energy. Crying out, he slithered wildly up through small, dark boulders that somehow clung to the mountain's face.

He knew it wouldn't be enough.

He could imagine the awful pain when those sharp fangs punctured his neck. He wondered if he would hear the crunch of bone, or if it would all be over before then. He wondered if the Good Lord could put all his parts together again so he and his pa could still ride a trail through a golden land someday.

Suddenly a deafening roar rocked the mountain. Fish spun to look right between the jaws of a man-killer. It was on top of him!

Pa! he cried silently. It's got me, Pa!

A powerful foreleg lashed out and slapped his calf, throwing him on his side. Suddenly he was in a sitting position, facing those gleaming fangs and trying to fend off its jaws with a boot. He caught the cat solidly in the nose, but the fangs still flashed. At the same instant he found a huge rock tottering at his ankle. With a vicious kick, he drove it hard right between the leaping jaguar's eyes.

The cat shrank back with a squall, and Fish turned and clawed at the rise. He found another big rock at arm's reach and sent it tumbling down as he scrambled past. He rolled a third rock in the jaguar's path, and a fourth.

Another roar blasted his ears, and a sledgehammer-of-a-paw caught him in the leg. He cried out and cast desperate eyes to a boulder just above. On a rim behind it sprawled two figures. They were lifting their boots against the jagged rock and fighting for leverage. Draped head-first over the rim's edge was a third figure that extended a frantic hand toward him.

With a last-gasp prayer, Fish lunged for those straining fingers.

· • ⟩ ∿ ⟨ • ·

Through the clasp of hands, Child-of-the-Waters felt the tug of the jaguar as it tried to drag his white brother away. Then the boulder beside the Apache boy was rocking, falling, rumbling. It was a mighty force that couldn't be denied. It missed the *pindah-lickoyee*'s leg by an arrow's width and bowled the cat over with crushing fury.

Suddenly fur was flying and so was the tiger. The hurtling boulder was carrying it right down the mountain!

Child-of-the-Waters felt like cheering. He wanted to shout taunts at that devil creature that abruptly lay so still on the trail below. But right now he had far more important matters to attend to.

As soon as he had reached this brief shoulder against the summit cliff, he had glimpsed the dark shadow at its base. Now as he helped his white brother to his feet, Child-of-the-Waters turned to study it.

At some point in time, the summit cap of boulders had partly collapsed. A flood of stone had roared down. It had stacked this small flat with big rocks and cluttered the slope with debris. Only a few yards ahead, a great pile of boulders climbed the face of the cliff all the way to the stacked heights.

Against the bluff leaned a huge, sun-splashed slab. He could see its shadow behind. Or did he? The sun's rays were coming in over his shoulder. With the sun at such an angle, it was impossible for the slab to throw that kind of a shadow.

He took a step toward it, and his white brother went with him. Now the crush of boulders moaned even more. There were plenty of crawl spaces between the rocks. Maybe part of what he heard was just the whistle of the wind. Still, the wail that came from that jag of darkness was like no wind he had ever known.

He wanted to run and hide. But Fish-Son-of-a-Cowboy was pressing ahead, and Child-of-the-Waters couldn't afford to be left behind.

Suddenly he knew the wail for what it was. These crags were the very cradle of life. All things had begun here, and maybe they would end here—sooner than anybody imagined. The mountain had been pierced, right to its heart. This very moment the blood of life was draining from this sacred place! When the lifeblood emptied, the Apaches would die as a people and everything would cease to be!

Yes, thought Child-of-the-Waters, these mountains had every reason to wail a mournful song of death.

He forced himself closer, trying to curb his fear. He had to give it his all, no matter what. Angry spirits, vengeful ghosts, disgrace in the eyes of the warriors—none of that mattered anymore. How could it? On his small shoulders rested not just his people's only hope, but maybe that of the whole world.

Behind the angled slab they found a partially blocked passage into the mountain. A chilled wind that seemed alive with those terrible, moaning spirits rushed from it. Or was this too just the whistling wind that sometimes lived in caverns?

The passage had the musty smell of a cave, but it was more than cave. The walls had chisel marks, as though it had been carved right out of the rock. Hewn timbers pushed against a low ceiling. Other timbers leaned at a bend far into the twilight. Still more marked the floor.

The two boys stepped inside, and a fine dust powdered up. They brushed through hanging cobwebs and were drawn to a ray of sunlight against the left wall. Suddenly Fish-Son-of-a-Cowboy was running trembling fingers along a glittering vein in the rock. He was talking excitedly and looking around for the other two white eyes.

Child-of-the-Waters shuddered.

He stood at *pesh-litzogue*, the place of the cursed yellow iron. Even now, he seemed to be able to feel the oozing lifeblood through the soles of his moccasins.

He spun and rushed past the other white eyes as they hurried in. Just before he reached the slab he saw a sizeable crawlway up through the boulder pile and took it. He slithered and wriggled, climbing a twisting course up through the heart of mighty rocks. He could feel the wind spirits in his face and hear their eerie groan.

The mass of boulders was a honeycomb of passages. But soon he squirmed into daylight and stood on a mound of rocks that crowned a mountain of mystery.

He seemed to be able to see forever. There were the island-like crags of the Chisos. There were the gaping canyons and the broken flats. There were the green forests and gray desert and the red-tinged del Carmens that sheltered his people the *Shis-Inday*.

There was earth and sky and life. And all of it might soon end if he didn't do his part.

He got the blessing of *Chigo-na-ay* the sun and whirled. All around him the hundred-foot jumble hung over the cliffs like a fat man's belly. But Child-of-the-Waters was searching for one boulder in particular. Oro had told him how the Apache slaves had worked to put it into place. For ninety-two winters, the stone had awaited the final push that would cause a landslide and close the mountain's wound. But upright boulders were everywhere along the rim! And they were so mighty! Even if he chose the right one, how could he ever dislodge it?

An Apache boy who believed himself the world's only hope scrambled up a wobbling boulder and looked straight down on *pesh-litzogue*.

CHAPTER 17

"**S**tart eatin', Punk!" Gid proclaimed gleefully.

"Huh?"

"That skunk sandwich! Slap it together and start chompin'! We done found us the mother lode of all gold mines!"

Fish had never been so excited. His heart was about to jump out of his chest. He was grinning and laughing and bouncing around as much as Gid was. Only Punk seemed subdued as he cast wary eyes at the entrance. Fish reckoned the wrangler just didn't like to be proved wrong. And boy, had he been wrong! They had found enough gold to buy half of Texas! Wait till they hauled some back to Papa Guy!

Fish gave the wrangler a playful nudge. "Come on, Punk! How come you ain't a-grinnin'? Didn't I tell you I knowed where it was at? I sure—"

"Shhh!" The wrangler lifted a hand for silence. "You yay-hoos are makin' so much racket, ol' Punk can't hear nothin'!"

"What are you listenin' for, Punk?" Gid asked, lowering his voice.

"It ain't Santy Claus, I'll tell you that! They's a mountain full of redskins out there somewheres!"

"But we lost 'em back at the bridge!" said Fish, hoping.

"Yeah? Well, you fellers didn't exactly tiptoe up here, did you? I been in stompedes that was quieter. Unless them Indians is deaf as my ol' grandma, they's fightin' right now like pigs over slop. You know, to see who gets whose hair."

Punk had a point, a mighty serious one. From what Child-of-the-Waters had said, those Apaches wanted this gold worse than they did. If those warriors had followed them here....

Fish shuddered. There had been no mistaking the Apache boy's gestures.

They'll draw their knives.

Outside the slab this very instant, eight fierce warriors could be doing just that. They could be headed straight their way, ready to claim this gold for themselves.

For a minute or two, Fish had forgotten some things. He had vowed to look but not touch, to find but not keep. But now the thought of what might be in store was setting him straight in a hurry.

He hadn't done an honest day's work for this gold, and it wasn't his to take.

The Good Book and his pa had both said so. To Fish, there could be no higher authorities.

"Say," whispered Punk, "speakin' of Indians, where'd that friend of yours run off to, anyhow?"

"I seen him shinnyin' up that hole yonder," said Gid, pointing. All at once he shivered. "You don't reckon he's gone off to bring back his kinfolk!"

Fish trusted Child-of-the-Waters. Twice now, the Apache boy had helped him out of bad scrapes. But he was still worried about all those warriors itching to take hold of his hair.

He swallowed hard and started for the jag of daylight that marked the entrance. "We...We gotta find out what's out there."

It took a lot of nerve for him to look outside that slab. It took even more to crawl out across that empty flat with Gid and Punk right behind. They sneaked right up to a big boulder on the rim and flattened themselves.

Fish's cheek brushed the rock as he began to peer around. A little at a time, the slope below came into view. Long before he could see it all, he cringed.

Several hundred feet down, a couple of bushes were gliding up the mountain. Or were they? Almost as soon as he thought so, they seemed rooted to the ground again.

"Did y'all see—"

All at once more shrubs seemed to start climbing.

"Them bushes is movin'!" Gid whispered.

"They's sprouted legs!" Punk added, lifting his head higher for a better look.

Fish knew what it was. His pa had fought plenty of Indians as a Texas Ranger. Apaches liked to sneak up by holding leafy branches as camouflage.

"Indians!" whispered Gid.

"Spots!" hollered Punk.

Suddenly the wrangler and Gid were bolting for the cave, leaving Fish lying there confused. Then he sprang up and saw what the boulder had hidden. Not forty feet below, the tiger was charging up the slope. The fall had only stunned it, and now its eyes burned fiercer than ever with devils!

He ran in panic after the youths and caught them just inside the slab. After the bright of day, the mine looked so gloomy, so...hopeless!

"There!" he cried, pointing. The crawlway up through the boulders looked too small for a tiger. Fish knew all about finding escape where a predator couldn't follow.

With a whoop and a whimper, Gid and Punk squeezed through. Fish was on their tails, diving in just as an ear-splitting roar shook the rock. Angry claws followed him, catching his boot long enough to terrify him. Then he was free and frantically wriggling up through the honeycomb passages.

At a bend the three of them stopped and turned. Fish almost expected to see shining eyes in the dark. He didn't, but they were still in an awful fix. That tiger had them pinned, and Apaches were on their way up to finish what the cat couldn't!

"What do we do, y'all?" he cried in a hushed voice.

They were close to the surface here, just a single layer of boulders away from the jumble's steep face. A pattern of sunlight filtered through the crevices. Fish had no sooner gotten the words out than a shadow blocked the light. A deep growl erupted and a huge foreleg shot in through a crack.

"Look out!" he cried, dodging a powerful swipe of claws.

"He's got us! He's got us!" exclaimed Gid.

The thing was pawing, slashing the air with those ripping claws. It was missing them by just inches!

Fish prodded the person in front of him. "Go, y'all! Go!"

They squirmed past the bend and on into the boulders' core. They slithered and climbed higher and higher through a maze that whispered with the ghostly wind. At a narrow opening that angled sharply upward, they hesitated. Just a few feet above, the passage ended at bright sky.

"Now what do we do!" Fish asked quietly.

"Them Indians is back there somewhere!" reminded Gid.

"Yeah, and ol' Spot's a durn sight closer than that!" added Punk, who was in the lead. He lifted his gaze to the daylight. "He's liable to be up yonder lickin' his chops! Ain't he seen how lank ol' Punk is? I need to go back and fatten up some, you measled-faced ball of hair!"

Fish hung his head. "I ... I guess this is my just deserts for ever wantin' that gold so bad. Oro tried to tell me it was cursed."

"Now you tell me!" chastised Gid. "Some brother you are! Here you been spoutin' that sign lingo with ever' Indian we meet, when I can't make heads or tails out of it! What else they told you that I don't know?"

"I ... I reckon I just didn't want to scare you off, Gid. I wanted you to come up here with me. But you go hidin' your head under the covers if ol' Grunt even tells a scary story."

"You ain't gonna make me any scareder now than I already am! So what's still to tell?"

Fish brushed a shaky hand across his face. "Oro was callin' this place the cradle of life. He said all life got started right there where that gold is. He said that mineral vein's kinda like a spring. Its power is what keeps ever'thing a-goin'—trees and birds and animals, even us.

"Anyhow, the Spaniards showed up. They made Oro and the Apaches go to minin' it. He said it was like openin' a vein in your arm. All that lifeblood that keeps ever'thing in the world alive went to oozin' out. It's still oozin'. That's just what he told me."

Fish felt a chill run down his back even as he was telling it. From the looks on Gid's and Punk's faces, they weren't exactly overcome with joy themselves.

"So why'd he send you chasin' off after it?" asked Gid.

"He was comin' back to heal up these mountains. He was gonna stop 'em from bleedin'. But he knew he'd never get here hisself. So he sent me."

"So what is it exactly he was wantin' a yay-hoo like you to do?" asked Punk.

"I don't know. He went and died on me."

"Well, that was durned rude of him," said the wrangler. "You reckon he—"

"Watch it, Punk!" Gid warned.

A dark shape was blotting out the patch of sky over the wrangler's head.

"It's that Indian boy!" Punk exclaimed. "He's wavin' ol' Punk up! What'll I do?"

"Go ahead!" said Fish. "He's my friend! Friends don't let each other down!"

In moments, the four boys stood on top of a mountain filled with danger. Child-of-the-Waters was pointing excitedly. He was making signs so fast that Fish had to slow him down. Even so, the words came in rapid-fire fashion.

"Help me! Help me!" Child-of-the-Waters seized Fish's arm and stared into his eyes. "Oro!" the Apache boy whispered frantically. "Oro the *izze-nantan*!"

"What about that old man?"

"The blood of life! It's running out of *pesh-litzogue*, the yellow iron cave! Didn't he tell you? The warriors—they'll make the wound a great river! They'll make it bleed like rushing waters! When the blood of life's gone—don't you see? Your people and the earth and sky—they will be no more!"

Fish now knew why Oro had looked so desperate that day in the desert.

"What is it you're wantin' me to do?" he pressed.

Child-of-the-Waters ran to a great boulder that perched on the rim right above the mine. Minutes before, he had climbed this lichen-covered rock and felt it move under his moccasins. Now he threw himself against it and the stone wobbled a little. Then he resumed his signs.

"The rock—we must roll it down! The yellow iron cave—we must cover it up! Don't you understand? The blood of life—it's pouring out! Our peoples will die! They'll all die! The *izze-nantan*—he sent you to heal this place! Help me! Please help me!"

Fish wasn't sure about all those Apache beliefs, but he knew one thing. That gold was cursed, like Oro had said. It had lured him here, and now they might die because of it. *That mine needed to stay hidden forever because of what it did to people!*

"We're in a bad way, fellers!"

Fish wheeled at Punk's cry. While Child-of-the-Waters had talked in signs, the wrangler and Gid had squeezed between boulders at the rim.

"Them redskins is plum' up to that trail already!" Punk added.

"Where's the tiger!" Fish cried.

"All I see's boulders down there!" blurted Gid. "You think—gosh! Oh my gosh! He come out from behind a rock near bottom! We gotta get outa here! He's comin' like blue blazes!"

But as Gid and Punk burst out of that squeeze, Fish seized their arms. Maybe all of them could have fled into those honeycomb passages again. But Child-of-the-Waters had made Fish realize they couldn't just run away. They had something to do—*the right thing!*

"Over yonder! That boulder—we gotta roll it down! It'll stop 'em! We gotta do it, y'all! We just gotta!"

He half-dragged them to the rock and joined Child-of-the-Waters in driving a shoulder into it.

"Push!" he cried. "Push with all you got!"

Suddenly four grunting boys were struggling desperately against a stubborn boulder that held their fates. Then a jaguar's bloodcurdling roar came rolling up the mountain.

"This thing ain't a-goin' nowhere!" hollered the wrangler. "But ol' Punk's a-fixin' to!"

"Stay with it, Punk!" Fish pleaded. "It's startin' to rock! Harder! Harder!"

"But they's a gold mine down there!" argued Gid, even as he strained with all his might. "Papa needs that gold!"

"He's like Pa! He don't want nothin' that ain't his! Come on, it's startin' to go! Just—one—more—

"There she goes! She's goin', y'all! Get away from it! Get away!"

The four of them reeled back as the great boulder went over the rim. Suddenly there was thunder and an earthquake. Fish could feel the rocks move right through his boots. But that didn't stop him from rushing to the rim and looking down.

Just yards below, the falling hunk of mountain barreled head-on into a brute shape. It had the body of a cat and the eyes of a devil. The jaguar was quick-footed and powerful, but it was up against a crushing force that couldn't be stopped.

The boulder flattened it and crashed on down the slope.

Suddenly the entire upper face of the mountain was collapsing. Tons of rocks were sliding and falling and thundering right down over the mine. The roar was louder than stampeding cattle or a Pecos twister. Through the raging dust, Fish could see the warriors whirling, fleeing, escaping.

The next thing he knew, the very rim where he stood was giving way.

"Get out of here!" he yelled, wheeling to run.

His cry was lost in the bedlam. But Gid and Punk didn't need any urging. They were already bolting for the back of the mountain.

Only Child-of-the-Waters hesitated. Hidden from the view of the warriors, he stared down on *pesh-litzogue*. It was like that day when *Usen* had made the world and scattered the leftover rocks here. The earth was shaking, rumbling, moaning. That day had given birth to the cradle of life and to a people called *Shis-Inday* Apaches. Ninety-two winters ago they had profaned this place and had begun to die. Now, with every crashing stone, Child-of-the-Water's people were finding new life. Soon they would be strong again, a mighty race!

"Come on!"

A hand seized his arm and pulled him away just as the rim collapsed. But now the summit itself was crumbling! It was dropping away at his feet! He had to run like *intchi-dijin* the black wind!

At the side of his white brother, Child-of-the-Waters fled with a smile.

CHAPTER 18

· •) 〰 (• ·

As soon as the four breathless boys crossed the swinging bridge, Gid and Punk ran for cover in the pinyon pines. But Child-of-the-Waters stopped Fish with a hand to his arm.

"I'll wait here for my people."

"You ain't goin' with us no further?" asked Fish, suddenly crushed. For the first time, he realized what a bond there was between them.

"I did what was right. But none of them must ever know. They'll come back this way and I'll go with them. We'll go back to our lodges and I'll be a warrior, not a boy. My people will be strong again, and someday I'll be a great war chief. But I'll never make war on a friend."

He put a hand on Fish's shoulder. "Thank you, my brother in battle. The mountain spirits will remember you even as you go away. They'll reward you and me and Oro. Someday we'll draw our last breaths and they'll bring us back to this place. They'll make us like the soaring rocks and mighty cliffs. They'll let us live side-by-side in these mountains forever. It's the way of the Chisos spirits."

"We're a team, ain't we," Fish said with a smile. "I reckon even them spirits know it now."

Then he lifted his clasped hands, making the first sign his pa had ever taught him.

"Friends!"

Turning, he fled into the timber.

· •) ≋ (• ·

All the way back to the ranch, Fish wondered what was to become of things.

Soon his Papa Guy might have to pull up stakes and move. His ma could be loading their belongings in a wagon right now. Before he knew it, he and Gid could be plowing the East Texas dirt and hoeing cotton.

It sure wasn't a life for a cowboy.

Still, Fish had no regrets. So what if he didn't have any gold to bring back! He had done what he had to back at that mountain. If the price for doing right meant giving up a few worldly things and starting over, then so be it. At least he and his family would still have each other.

The three boys put ten miles of desert between them and the mountains before the green willows at headquarters came into view. The moment they pulled rein at the simple box-and-plank house, Papa Guy and Mama Elizabeth came running out. Fish expected a lot of frowns from his ma and a good licking from Papa Guy. But the gaunt woman and the leathery-faced man had other ideas. They wrapped Fish and Gid up in their arms the moment the boys climbed off their horses.

Papa Guy was lean, tanned, and tough, the way a cowboy should be. But he was plenty misty-eyed as he withdrew and looked them over.

"Gosh a-mighty, am I glad to see y'all! I just rode in from New Mexico not ten minutes ago! I was fixin' to grab some grub and head out lookin' for you! Your Mama Elizabeth was plum' sure y'all had been scalped!"

"Durn near!" spoke up Punk. "Scalped and drownded and gobbled up by hungry hair balls—you name it! Say, next time you fellers go traipsin' off in them mountains, I'll be a-thinkin' about you over a plate of beans."

"They ain't gonna have time for that for a while, Punk," said Guy. "You either."

"How come, Papa?" asked Gid.

"I'll be needin' a couple of good trail hands and a wrangler. That Yankee fort up the Pecos wants all the steers I can bring 'em."

"Really, Papa Guy?" Fish asked excitedly.

"You bet. We'll be comin' back with enough Yankee dollars to build your mama the kinda house we all been needin'."

Fish looked at his ma and suddenly felt all kinds of joy. He had a real family again, and now his tomorrows looked even better! But at the same time, he thought about all his yesterdays. A lot had happened since he had started west nearly two years ago. Some of it had been bad, but more of it had been good. He had lost his pa, all right. But he had also learned an awful lot about life.

It wasn't that hard to understand, really. It had to do with faith in the Good Lord, trust in his fellow man, and courage. Sometimes it took all three to do what was right and not worry about the consequences.

But life was also about people.

In Fish's case, there were his pa and ma, who would always ride with him. There were Gid and Papa Guy, who had welcomed him into their family. And there were his friends—Punk, Hunting Bear, Child-of-the-Waters.

And how could he ever forget a dying old Apache who had involved him in mysteries he still didn't understand?

"Funny I ain't never noticed that before."

Fish turned at Papa Guy's voice.

"What is it, Papa?" asked Gid.

"Them mountains yonder. The Chisos. See how them things is shaped on top? See how they make a nose and chin and forehead against the horizon?"

Fish stared at those eerie crags that were also a part of his life now.

"The way it's layin' there lookin' up at the sky," said Papa Guy, "doggoned if it don't remind me of a—"

"Indian!" Fish exclaimed in sudden awe.

It looked like Oro!

THE END

· • ） ≈ （ • ·

The Legend Behind the Story

The Chisos Mountains in present-day Big Bend National Park of Texas have always seemed mysterious. Like an island, they rise more than a mile out of the vast Chihuahuan Desert. In the dusk, their many crags and rock towers look like spirits rising out of a mist.

The very name "Chisos" speaks of mystery. Some people believe it comes from the Spanish word *hechizo*—"bewitched" —or an Indian word meaning "ghosts."

Legends of hidden treasure in the Chisos go back a long way. "The people of the Big Bend region have a tradition that in the days of the Spanish [rule],... convicts were kept and worked in

Close-up of Lost Mine Peak in Chisos Mountains. (photo by author)

Lost Mine Peak in the Chisos as seen across Juniper Canyon. (photo by author)

certain mythical mines in the Chisos Mountains," wrote explorer
Robert T. Hill in 1899.

Indeed, Spanish officials sent conquistadors in search of gold
in the Southwest. At the same time, they wanted to conquer this
new land. To do so, they had to take measures against war-loving
Indians such as Comanches and Apaches.

The first step was to build a line of forts along New Spain's
northern frontier. One of these was Presidio de San Vicente. It
was set up in 1773 just inside present Mexico and eighteen miles
southeast of the Chisos. By 1781 the Spaniards had abandoned
the fort—but not before finding gold in the Chisos.

Or so the story goes, anyway.

Juan Gamboa heard a lot of tales about the mine when he
moved to a village near Presidio de San Vicente in 1923. He
related:

"Back in the old days the Indians made horseshoes from silver. In the Chisos Mountains in Big Bend National Park there is a mine which the Spaniards worked. The mine is said to have been directly across from the presidio mission. The Spaniards used Indian labor and blindfolded them to and from the mission. From the mission there was a tunnel to the river which the Spaniards used to keep from being attacked by Indians. That tunnel is still hid or buried somewhere. There was a bridge made of wood across a very deep canyon, or crevice, which separated the mine from the outside."

James Owens heard more details when he lived in the Chisos in the mid-1930s.

"They worked Indians in those mines and they'd never come out—they'd work them to death. They were the Apaches, and so they rebelled. They cornered these Mexicans [or Spaniards] with twenty jackloads [donkey-loads] of gold or silver up there in one of those box canyons in the Chisos, and killed them all. And then they ran these jacks over the side of the cliff. And to get out of the canyon themselves, they had to climb the cliffs. The Indians were able to escape, and they created a tremendous rockslide in the process; they did it deliberately. And it covered over the Lost Chisos Mine."

Dreamers have searched for the Spanish diggings for more than a century. An old story claims that if a person stands in the doorway of Presidio de San Vicente's mission at sunrise on Easter, he will see a vital clue. The first rays of the rising sun will strike the Chisos either at the mine's entrance or at the top of the peak that holds the mine at its base.

In the 1930s Owens heard a slightly different version.

"You can stand in the old mission at San Vicente in the afternoon [of a certain day] in August, and whenever the sun goes down, it's supposed to go down between two peaks. And at the base of those peaks is where this mine exists."

Despite such clues, the Chisos Mountains so far have refused to give up their secrets. But that doesn't keep people from looking and dreaming. Each year thousands hike the Lost Mine Trail in Big Bend National Park in search of a legend. If you make a trip to Big Bend, be sure to include this trail on your list of things to do. Also, drive north on Grapevine Hills Road and look back at

Alsate's Profile in the Chisos Mountains.
(photo by author)

the Chisos. You'll see a mountain formation that looks like the face of an Indian staring at the sky. It's known as "Alsate's Profile."

Maybe it should be called "Oro's Profile."

For more information on the Lost Chisos Mine, see *Portraits of the Pecos Frontier* by Patrick Dearen. For other treasure tales of Texas, see *Coronado's Children* by J. Frank Dobie, and *Castle Gap and the Pecos Frontier* by Patrick Dearen.

For a history of the Big Bend, read *The Big Bend: A History of the Last Texas Frontier* by Ron C. Tyler. Also see the video *Bandits, Bootleggers, and Businessmen: The History of the Big Bend 1848-1948* (Forest Glen Productions, Inc., P.O. Box 101823, Fort Worth, Texas 76185-1823). Another good visual study of the Big Bend is the video *The Spiral Dance: Reflections on Big Bend National Park*, produced by the Chihuahuan Desert Research Institute.

For information about Apaches, see *The People Called Apache* by Thomas E. Mails, and *The Apaches: Eagles of the Southwest* by Donald E. Worcester.

If you have trouble finding any of these titles, ask the interlibrary loan department at your local public library for help.

· •) ≈ (• ·